JENNIFER BLECHER

Stick with Me

BEST FRIENDS

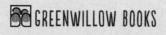

GREENWILLOW BOOKS

AN IMPRINT OF HARPERCOLLINS*PUBLISHERS*

Stick With Me

Text copyright © 2020 by Jennifer Blecher. Illustrations copyright © 2020 by Celia Krampien.

www.harpercollinschildrens.com

The text of this book is set in Revival 555 BT. Book design by Sylvie Le Floc'h

Library of Congress Cataloging-in-Publication Data

Names: Blecher, Jennifer, author.
Title: Stick with me / Jennifer Blecher.
Description: First edition. | New York, NY : Greenwillow Books, an Imprint of HarperCollins Publishers, [2020] | Audience: Ages 8-12. | Audience: Grades 4-6.
Summary: When twelve-year-olds Izzy and Wren are thrown together by unusual circumstances, they find solace and solutions to nagging problems in their newly-formed friendship.
Identifiers: LCCN 2020017523 (print) | ISBN 9780062748638 (paperback)
Subjects: CYAC: Best friends—Fiction. | Friendship—Fiction. |Theater—Fiction. | Ice skating—Fiction. | Family life—Fiction.
Classification: LCC PZ7.B61658 Sti 2020 (print) | DDC [Fic] —dc23
LC record available at https://lccn.loc.gov/2020017523

21 22 23 24 25 PC/BRR 10 9 8 7 6 5 4 3 2 1

First Greenwillow paperback, 2021

Greenwillow Books

TO JEFF

THE OPPOSITE OF IZZY

When Izzy was little, she was obsessed with opposites. Not regular opposites, like left and right. Happy and sad. Good and bad. She wasn't the kind of kid who occasionally walked down the sidewalk backward. Instead, Izzy blew milk out of a straw. She ate cereal with a fork. She wore her backpack on her stomach every single day of preschool.

It didn't make any sense.

But back then, making sense didn't matter. Izzy could color only the background of a coloring page, and her teacher would smile and say, "What a unique way to look at that picture, Izzy. You did such a nice job coloring *outside* the lines."

And it wasn't just teachers. No one in her family cared about making sense. If Izzy danced around the kitchen with underwear on her head, there was an excellent chance that her parents would laugh. Or that her older brother Nate would twirl her down the hallway.

But now Izzy was twelve. And that kind of stuff wasn't funny anymore; it was embarrassing. Izzy no longer wanted to be different from everyone else.

She wanted the opposite.

As Izzy sat at her desk watching her friend Phoebe, she got a familiar feeling, like things were the opposite of how they were supposed to be. Only the feeling didn't make Izzy smile or laugh. It made her worry about what was going to happen next.

"I'm not sure I get it," said Phoebe. Phoebe was lying on Izzy's bed. Her feet swayed in the air and her head rested in her palms. Four beaded bracelets slid halfway down Phoebe's arm. They were the same bracelets that Daphne Toll, the most popular girl in class, had started wearing a few months ago.

There were real bracelets and there were fake bracelets. The real bracelets were made of colored stones threaded on a thick elastic band. The fake bracelets looked exactly the same, but instead of stones, they were made with heavy plastic beads. The only way to tell which bracelets were real and which were fake was to listen to the sound the bracelets made when they hit one another or a hard surface.

Daphne's bracelets were real. Izzy sat next to Daphne in English and had to listen as Daphne clacked her bracelets together during silent reading time. Phoebe's bracelets were fake. Phoebe's mom had bought them in the "buy three, get one free" section at Glitz.

But Izzy had never told anyone that. And neither had Phoebe.

Real and fake. Opposites.

"Earth to Izzy," said Phoebe. She waved her hand with the bracelets back and forth. "Hel-lo."

"Sorry," said Izzy. "What'd you say?"

"I said, I don't get this sticker door. What's the point? What were we *thinking*?" Phoebe nodded toward the back of Izzy's bedroom door. It was covered with hundreds of stickers. There were heart stickers, puppy stickers, and unicorn stickers. There was a winding path of stars, fuzzy ducks wearing red rain boots, and grinning cows jumping over full moons. Around the doorknob was a swirl of whales, seahorses, and sharks. Toward the top of the door were smiling pieces of sushi, old-fashioned dolls wearing lace bonnets, and neon skulls with empty eye sockets. The bottom of the door was lined with neat rows of emoji stickers.

Izzy and Phoebe used to stare at the masterpiece that they'd created together and imagine stories about the lives of the stickers. *Green neon skull and doll in a lace bonnet had a baby named poop emoji.* That kind of thing.

Izzy shrugged. "We were thinking that it was fun?"

"I guess," said Phoebe. "But I just don't get it anymore. I don't get the point."

"There wasn't a point."

"There has to be a point, Izzy. Otherwise, what's the point?"

This was how Phoebe spoke now that she hung out with Daphne and all her popular friends. Now that she wore a stack of bracelets on her wrist and sat at Daphne's table in the cafeteria, draping her arms and legs over Daphne so that everyone could see how deeply connected they were. Now that she spun her lacrosse stick in her hand as she walked to the playing fields for practice, her ponytail held back with a navy-blue elastic headband just like every other girl on the team.

Everything had to *mean* something. And the most annoying part was, Phoebe never knew what anything meant. She just liked to wonder about it.

Like what did it *mean* that Zach bumped into her when Phoebe was putting away her iPad in science? What did it *mean* that Serena went to Dr. Forte's office on Thursday afternoon? What did it *mean* that Mr. Blair picked Phoebe last to give her presentation in English?

Here's what Izzy wanted to know: What did it *mean* that Phoebe, who'd had tons of sleepovers in Izzy's bedroom, was looking around the room like she'd never seen it before? What did it *mean* that watching Phoebe pull at the frayed knees of her jeans made Izzy wonder if her splatter-paint leggings were babyish? What did it *mean* that having Phoebe close by made Izzy feel lonelier than actually being alone?

Phoebe sat up on Izzy's bed and crossed her legs. Her bare knee popped through the hole in her jeans. "Should we find our moms?" Phoebe asked. "They're probably done talking by now."

So I can finally go home. Those were the words Phoebe didn't say. Although they both knew that the only reason Phoebe was at Izzy's house was because their moms wanted to catch up over a cup of tea.

Phoebe's mom and Izzy's mom were best friends. Sometimes Izzy imagined their moms like a drawing in a picture book: two smiling girls holding hands against a white background with the words BEST FRIENDS written underneath in thick black text. That's all the page would say, as if having a best friend was the simplest thing in the world. As if everyone had a best friend necklace from Glitz, the kind with two jagged half hearts on separate chains that fit together to make a whole.

When they were little, Phoebe and Izzy had been best friends, too. They had half-heart necklaces. They'd gone to the mall and picked them out before their first day of kindergarten. Their moms took their picture, told them how adorable they were, and bought them strawberry ice cream cones to celebrate. Because that's how things worked back then. Necklaces formed hearts. There weren't real hearts and fake hearts. There were just two halves that fit together to make a whole.

Izzy didn't know exactly when everything changed, or why. But she was certain that two simple words no longer described her and Phoebe. Their friendship wasn't just building fairy houses, or performing dance routines on summer nights while their parents ate dinner in the backyard, or making slime creations speckled with silver glitter. It was birthday parties where Izzy was no longer the one seated right next to Phoebe when Phoebe blew out the candles on her cake, school pickups where Phoebe piled into cars heading to houses that Izzy had never been invited to, and beaded bracelets and lacrosse team headbands that Phoebe wore daily and Izzy did not own.

That this change had happened slowly didn't make it any less confusing. If anything, Izzy wished that there had been something specific, like when they were little and Izzy had stuck a heart sticker on the belly of Phoebe's stuffed bunny named Carrot because she thought it would make Phoebe happy. Phoebe had been the opposite of happy, especially when she ripped the sticker off and discovered that it had left behind a sticky gray goo that matted Carrot's pink fur. As Phoebe sat on the kitchen floor with tears and snot streaming down her face, Izzy and her mom had soaked Carrot in a bucket of warm soapy water until the sticker goo came off. Then Izzy and Phoebe spent the rest of the day playing animal spa, bathing their favorite stuffed animals and laying them in the sun to dry.

By dinnertime, they were begging their moms to let them have a sleepover.

Izzy almost smiled, remembering how they brought their stuffed animals ripe blueberries stacked onto toothpicks and bowed as they presented the delicate treats. But then Izzy realized that she had no idea if Phoebe still slept with Carrot tucked under her arm. If she still chewed on Carrot's long ears when she was nervous, or threw Carrot against the wall when she was frustrated. How long had it been since Izzy had seen Carrot's large feet and black stitched grin? Months? Maybe even a whole year?

Phoebe rolled off Izzy's bed, examined her nails, and sighed. "Come on," she said. "Let's go."

"One sec," said Izzy. She swiveled her chair so that her back was to Phoebe and glanced at the drawer of her desk. Her half of their jagged heart necklace was inside. But there was something else inside, too. A stack of papers that Izzy didn't want Phoebe, or anyone else, to see.

"Come on, Iz," said Phoebe. "I'm starving."

A piece of striped washi tape was stuck across the panel of the drawer, sealing it shut. The top edge of the tape was beginning to curl away and Izzy was tempted to reach out and fix it. But there was no way to do that without Phoebe noticing. Phoebe would wonder what the tape *meant*.

And even Phoebe was smart enough to know the answer.

Izzy stood up and followed Phoebe out of her bedroom toward the back stairway. As they walked, Phoebe dragged her hand with the stack of beaded bracelets along the white hallway wall. Izzy almost told Phoebe to stop. Izzy's mom was always reminding Izzy and Nate to be careful about leaving fingerprints on the walls. But she worried that Phoebe would just roll her eyes. And Izzy had no clue what she'd do then.

Thankfully, Phoebe raised her hand to flip her hair and gather it over her shoulder. The hair flip was a classic Daphne move. Izzy had tried to draw the motion on paper. The key to getting it right was in the head tilt and upturned eyes. But the faces Izzy drew always looked deep in thought, as if they were pondering the mysteries of the universe.

The opposite of what the expression looked like in real life.

They were almost to the bottom of the stairway when Phoebe stopped and pressed one finger to her lips. Izzy nodded. Phoebe's hunched shoulders and wide grin made Izzy feel like they were still little and wearing their jagged half-heart necklaces. Izzy was relieved that she hadn't said anything about fingerprints. This moment wouldn't have happened if she had.

Leaning with their backs against the stairway wall, they heard Phoebe's mom say, "I'm so sorry. That's really tough."

"We'll figure something out," said Izzy's mom. "I'm working on a few ideas."

"How's Greg handling it?" asked Phoebe's mom.

"You can imagine," said Izzy's mom.

Silence.

What would her mom figure out? What ideas was she

working on? Izzy leaned forward to peek around the corner. But Phoebe pressed Izzy back against the wall, as if they were about to hear something interesting and she didn't want Izzy to ruin the moment.

Greg was Izzy's dad. He fixed whatever was broken in their house—rattling pipes, flickering lights, loose-hinged doors that scraped the hardwood floors. Izzy's house was super old and her parents had spent years fixing it up. They'd torn down walls, ripped up tile, and peeled off wallpaper. Izzy's mom once spent an entire week polishing the doorknobs and window locks to restore their original color. So maybe that's what her mom was talking about?

But as the silence in the kitchen continued, Izzy began to worry that her mom was talking about something way more serious than home repairs.

Suddenly Phoebe jumped from the stairway to the kitchen floor. She landed with a thump.

"Phoebe," said Phoebe's mom. "You scared me."

"What were you guys talking about?" asked Phoebe.

"Nothing," said Izzy's mom. She stood up from

her stool and pressed her fingers against the corners of her eyes. *Was she about to cry?*

"Mom," said Izzy. "What's wrong?"

"Um, I think I might be getting a cold. It's terrible timing." Izzy's mom reached for a tissue. But instead of blowing her nose, she crumpled the tissue in her hand.

Izzy's mom was starting an interior-design business. Her first potential client was coming over that afternoon to see their house and get a sense of her mom's style. All afternoon she'd been plumping pillows, refolding blankets, and straightening picture frames. Even then, Izzy's mom stuffed the tissue in her pocket and looked around the kitchen like she was searching for a spill to wipe clean.

Phoebe picked a red grape from the ceramic bowl in the center of the island. She peeled off the skin before popping the grape in her mouth.

"Are you girls hungry?" asked Izzy's mom as she scrubbed an invisible spot on the counter. "I have some frozen cookie dough in the freezer. I was going to put it in the oven later to give the house a homey smell, but I can do it now."

"Good idea," said Phoebe's mom. "What do you say, Phoebe? Want to stay for some cookies?"

Phoebe reached for another grape. "No, thanks. I'll eat at my sleepover."

"Oh," said Izzy's mom. "Okay." She glanced at Phoebe's mom.

Phoebe's mom shrugged, but just barely. As if maybe Izzy wouldn't notice.

Izzy hated how clueless they thought she was. About the cookie bribe. The shrug. The sleepover at Daphne's house that Izzy already knew about because she'd heard girls talking about it at school. The fact that Phoebe was suddenly not hungry even though she said she was starving a few minutes ago and kept reaching for grapes.

Izzy knew their moms wished that she and Phoebe were still babies so they could plop them down on a soft blanket with some squeaking toys and continue talking. But life wasn't that simple anymore. Phoebe had places to go. And Izzy was not invited.

◆◆◆

Izzy pressed her forehead against the cold glass of her bedroom window and watched as Phoebe and her mom backed down the driveway. When Izzy moved her head away, there was an oval shape where the warmth of her breath had clouded the glass. With her finger, Izzy drew a heart in the condensation. Then she slashed the heart in half with a zigzag streak.

Sitting down at her desk with a clean piece of paper, Izzy reached for the tin container where she kept her Sharpies. The tin was a deep teal color with delicate white butterflies etched on the sides. Her mom had bought it at a tea shop in London before Izzy was born. The sides were dented, and one of the butterfly's wings had worn completely off. But it was Izzy's favorite possession. She loved that the tin was the perfect size for her Sharpies, and the pinging sound each Sharpie made when she dropped it inside.

Izzy chose a violet Sharpie and drew a flower with different circles of looping petals. But her hand slipped when she tried to add detail to the stem. Izzy tore the page in half and tossed it on the floor.

She looked at the window. The condensation had evaporated, but her fingertip left smudged streaks on the glass. Great. Now she was stuck with one jagged heart in her desk and another one on her window.

Phoebe would probably love to know what that *meant*.

Izzy didn't want to think about Phoebe. That was a mistake, just like her hand slipping. Only there was no mess-up pile for bad thoughts. Bad drawings she could tear in half and throw away. Bad thoughts got trapped inside Izzy's head. It wasn't like she could just ask Phoebe why she was ditching her all the time. Phoebe would look at her like the answer was so obvious that it couldn't even be put into words. And then Izzy would feel even worse.

Izzy grabbed a fresh piece of paper and her black Sharpie from the butterfly tin. She drew a simple stick-figure girl. On top of the figure's straight-line neck, Izzy drew a round head with long hair and wide eyes.

She added eyebrows, a navy elastic headband, and rosy cheeks. Next, in alternating colors, Izzy drew a stack of bracelets around the stick figure's wrist. Picking up the black Sharpie again, Izzy added a large bubble coming from the stick figure's mouth with the words: WHY DON'T YOU GET SOME NEW FRIENDS?

Izzy almost left it like that, but there was too much blank space on the page that needed to be filled. She chose the brown Sharpie and drew a jagged mountain edge beginning at the stick figure's feet. Toward the top of the mountain Izzy added some wildflowers. But as her hand moved down the mountain, Izzy found herself turning the wildflowers into sharp-tipped spikes.

There was no denying it: the stick figure looked like Phoebe. And one gentle push would send her crashing right over the mountain's spike-filled edge.

When the drawing was done, the letters in the word bubble highlighted, and the mountain decorated with gray rocks and occasional sprouts of green grass, Izzy lifted it to eye height. The light from her bedroom window brought out the paper's texture and gave the scene depth, as if the mountain was surrounded by a wintery haze.

And finally, the thoughts in Izzy's head settled like flakes in a snow globe. They were still there, but they were quieter, as if some of the hurt and loneliness and fear that things would never get better had escaped into the crisp, saturated lines of her Sharpies.

Izzy tore off the striped washi tape and opened the drawer of her desk. She placed the drawing on top of the growing pile. Then she ripped off a new piece of washi tape from the roll and sealed the drawer shut.

WATCH WREN FLY

"Okay, Bird," said Wren's dad. "Let's see you fly."

Wren pushed off from the ice-skating rink boards. The edges of her blades carved into the frozen surface. With every stroke, Wren skated faster.

The cold, early morning air rushed over her cheeks, across her neck, and between each individual finger.

Wren inhaled. It tasted crisp, like spearmint gum.

She turned into her back crossovers, her arms wide and her legs moving in smooth inside-edged arcs.

She gathered speed. And power.

Wren waited for the click in her brain that told

her it was time. When it came, Wren balanced on her right leg, gliding backward while she prepared the rest of her body. Shoulders down. Head high. Arms back.

She stepped forward onto her bent left leg and pushed off until the toe pick on the tip of her skate blade caught in the ice.

Wren swung her body forward.

She lifted into the cold air. Where she heard nothing. Saw nothing.

Wren was flying, floating, spinning.

Two-and-a-half turns later, she landed backward on her right leg. A double axel.

The muffled sound of her dad clapping his leather-gloved hands echoed across the ice. "That's my Bird!" he shouted. "Woo-hoo!"

Wren held her landing position for the count of five. Then she turned forward and skated back to the boards.

"Amazing," said her dad. "You made that double axel look like a piece of cake."

"It's not," said Wren, her hands on her hips, catching her breath.

"Well, it sure looked that way." Wren's dad raised his fist and she bumped it with her own. Then he checked his watch. Before he could say anything, Wren skated away.

Her legs were the perfect combination of warm and strong. Her body wanted to fly again.

The feeling was like a gentle poke deep inside her brain. A combination of mental and physical. Brain and body.

It was everything working together, under her command.

She could jump. Axel, lutz, toe loop, flip, salchow.

Or spin. Layback, camel, sit, scratch.

She could stretch into a graceful spiral, or switch into a fast-paced footwork section.

On the ice, Wren was in charge.

Her dad could check his watch. Then his phone. He could cross his arms over his chest or fiddle with his wool hat.

What was he going to do? Chase her across the ice in his snow boots?

Wren's dad was the men's ice hockey coach at Dartmouth College. He knew how rare it was for her to have the entire ice rink to herself. It only happened early in the morning when the hockey teams were on a rest day. Wren's dad would use his coach's key to unlock the ice rink door and they would stand together in the dark as the overhead lights flickered on with loud buzzes and electric clicks.

At other times there were skaters who Wren needed to watch out for. Younger kids practicing waltz jumps who didn't have the speed and coordination to get out of her way. Older teenagers who left deep divots in the ice that she had to avoid.

So Wren didn't want to get off the ice until she had no choice. Until the huge rubber wheels of the Zamboni machine began their slow churn across the frozen surface, Charlie behind the wheel yelling at Wren to clear out already.

Yelling, but also smiling.

When Wren was younger, Charlie would let her sit on the bench of the Zamboni while her dad led his team through endless drills and her mom stayed home with Wren's little sister, Hannah.

"You like the view from up here?" Charlie had asked one day.

Wren had nodded. She'd gripped the cold metal Zamboni wheel with both hands, pretending to steer with exaggerated movements.

"Just you wait till you see the view of the ice from the winner's podium," Charlie continued. "That's where a skater like you should be."

Wren glanced up at him. "Me?"

"You see any other pint-size people working harder? You got fire in your belly, kid."

Then Charlie ruffled Wren's hair, which she hated, before climbing down to shovel the slushy pile of ice remains.

Wren had always been aware of it. A restless stirring. An energy that wanted her to move fast. Jump high. Spin tight.

Now the sensation had a name: fire in her belly. And Wren loved it.

She entered competitions at her rink, skating short programs to happy, chipper music. A waltz jump here. A sit spin there. Pink ribbons fluttered in her braided pigtails and wide smiles displayed missing teeth. Wren stepped onto podiums barely higher than a shoebox and bent her head as plastic medals were placed around her neck.

But then things began to change.

The competitions got farther away. They were held on ice surfaces that were harder or softer, at rinks with overhead lights that were too bright or too dim. Wren started skating against girls who wanted to stand on the podium just as much as she did.

The fire in her belly remained. But it got harder and harder to win.

Which is why no matter how many times her dad glanced at his watch, Wren wouldn't get off the ice. The only other time she had an entire ice surface to herself was during competitions. She'd been over it one hundred times and decided that was why she blew it at sectionals last year.

She let the empty ice rattle her. She lost track of her music. She lost her focus.

And on the final double lutz in her program, Wren fell.

Laney Lewis got the bronze.

Laney Lewis got to stand on the podium and compete at nationals in San Francisco against the top skaters in the country.

Wren got fourth.

There was no place on the podium for fourth. Fourth was not special. It took her nowhere.

Wren refused to let that happen again. This year she was going to place in the top three at sectionals and qualify for nationals.

Sectionals was just four weeks away. It was time to push harder than ever before.

"Seriously, Bird," yelled her dad as he pulled his cell phone from the pocket of his jeans and frowned. "We've gotta go."

"Just one run-through of my program," said Wren. "Charlie's not even here yet to warm up the Zamboni."

Wren didn't wait for her dad to respond. She skated to center ice and struck her opening pose. Gaze down. Arms overhead.

From the corner of her eye, she saw her dad shake his head and walk to the rink's sound system, cueing up her program music.

As the electric opening beats of her music played, Wren's dad yelled, "Just once. Your mom and Hannah are waiting. So after this, it's straight off the ice."

Wren nodded, but she tried to put his words out of her mind.

All she wanted to think about were her jumps, spins, and footwork sequences.

She tried to hear only the music. Feel only her body.

But Wren couldn't get in the zone. Something was off. When it came time for her double lutz, she under-rotated. The blade on her landing foot made contact at the wrong angle. Wren crashed to the ice.

She picked herself right up. She increased the pace of her forward crossovers to catch up with the music and ended her program with a strong double axel. But when Wren stepped off the ice and slid her plastic skate guards over her blades, she noticed the weight of her boots and the effort it took to move her tired legs to the locker room.

And she allowed herself to think it. Even though she hated the thought.

Thanks a lot, Hannah. This is all your fault.

Inside Lou's Restaurant and Bakery it was warm and sweet, as if the sugary icing that coated Lou's famous cinnamon buns was floating in the air. Wren unzipped her fleece skating jacket. She followed her dad to a booth in the back of the bakery where her mom and four-year-old Hannah were hunched over pieces of paper, coloring with crayons.

Wren's dad put his finger to his lips and snuck up to them, surprising Wren's mom with a kiss on the lips.

Wren expected her mom to swat him away. Or look embarrassed.

Instead, she reached her hands around his neck and gave him a long kiss.

"Eww," said Hannah.

"You're next," said their dad. He stepped toward Hannah with his arms wide, like a pretend monster. As Hannah squealed, he planted a sloppy kiss on her cheek and straightened the paper crown that was tilted on her head. Then he folded his large body into the booth beside Hannah. Wren slid in beside her mom.

"Good skate?" asked Wren's mom.

"I missed my double lutz," said Wren. "Again."

"That's okay. You'll get it."

"It's not okay. I keep under-rotating."

Wren paused, waiting for her mom to ask if her dad had caught the fall on video. Maybe she could take a look? Try to figure out what went wrong?

Twice a week Wren took skating lessons with a professional coach named Nancy. But Nancy charged by the hour and taught several students a day. She didn't have the time to sit and watch Wren's jumps in slow motion, analyzing the angle of her blade and the position of her shoulders.

But Wren's mom did. When Wren was having a tough time with a new jump, her mom would stand in the bleachers and video Wren's practices. After Wren finished her homework, they'd sit together on the couch and watch the recording.

They'd zoom in, looking for a shoulder tilted at the wrong angle. A foot lifted too high. An arm that released too late.

Sometimes, after watching Wren fall over and over, her mom would say that what they really needed was to watch puppy videos on YouTube.

And then try again tomorrow.

As Wren sat in the booth at Lou's waiting for her mom to offer to help, she realized it had been weeks since they'd watched puppy videos.

Wren understood why. She knew those videos weren't important.

But that didn't make her miss those silly puppies

getting their heads stuck in trash cans any less.

"Wren," said Hannah, tapping Wren's hand across the table. "Do you like my new crown?"

Wren nodded. "Yeah. It's really pretty. Are you going to a royal ball?"

Hannah shook her head. The paper crown slid down her forehead. "It's not a princess crown. It's for meeting unicorns."

"Unicorns?" asked Wren, looking from Hannah to her mom.

Hannah smiled. "Yep."

"Wait, what?" said Wren's dad. He tried to stand, but his thighs hit the underside of the table. Forks and knives jumped. A water glass spilled. "Did Dr. Koffer call?"

Wren's mom smiled. "Her nurse called while you were at the rink. Dr. Koffer reviewed all Hannah's tests and she thinks she can help. She had an unexpected cancellation next week. I think we should take it. Otherwise it could be months before she can see us."

Wren's dad slid out of the booth. He lifted Hannah

into his arms and began jumping in place. Hannah's crown fell over her eyes.

Wren's mom raised her phone to take a picture. "Look at me, you two. Smile."

Three college kids in the booth next to them turned and stared. But only Wren noticed. She grabbed some napkins from the dispenser and cleaned up the spilled water.

This was the news that Wren's parents had been waiting for. Hannah had epilepsy, which meant that her brain had seizures. Sometimes the seizures made Hannah's arms go stiff, or her eyes wander, or her body shake. The seizures were usually fast, but when they happened, it felt like they lasted forever.

In the year since the seizures began, Hannah had tried three different kinds of medication to make them stop. None of the medicines worked. So a few weeks ago, Hannah and her mom went to a hospital in Boston to meet with a new team of doctors.

They stayed in the hospital for an entire week. Wren stayed home with her dad.

Every night her dad's phone pinged with texts from her mom. Pictures of Hannah playing with therapy dogs, or banging on drums with a music teacher, or squeezing the red rubber nose of a clown.

Wren had leaned over her dad's shoulder as he swiped through the photos. But she barely noticed the shaggy golden retrievers. The shiny cymbals. The clown's exaggerated smile.

All she could focus on were the red, blue, and yellow wires running down Hannah's head. They were stuck to Hannah's scalp with round stickers and told the doctors what part of Hannah's brain was causing the seizures.

That's where Dr. Koffer came in. She specialized in the kind of surgery that Hannah needed. Her job was to cut out the section of Hannah's brain that was causing the seizures.

Not that Wren's family used words like *surgery* and *cut*. Words that were too hard to say out loud.

Instead, they used *unicorn* as a code name for Hannah's treatment. Their parents told Hannah that having epilepsy made her extra special, like how a unicorn would just be a horse without its magical horn. They said that if Hannah went to all her doctor's appointments and tests, maybe she'd get to do something really amazing, like meet an actual unicorn.

Wren thought the code name was stupid. It made no sense.

Special was good. Special was people cheering your name as you stood on the top of a podium.

Epilepsy was scary. Watching Hannah have a seizure reminded Wren of catching her toe pick in the ice, the moment of knowing she was about to fall but being unable to prevent it. Except Wren could handle a bruised knee. A sore hip. Hannah was so little and helpless.

But whatever, Wren's parents thought the unicorn comparison was brilliant. It stuck.

Maggie, their favorite waitress at Lou's, came up to their table. She raised one eyebrow. "What exactly are you all so happy about over here?" asked Maggie. "Did this dynamo of ours add another skating medal to her collection?"

Wren's mom shook her head, unable to answer. She put her phone down on the table, looked at Hannah, and started crying. Messy, snotty, emotional tears.

"Noooo," said Maggie, glancing from Wren's mom to Hannah. "Does this mean what I think it means?"

"It does," said Wren's dad. "It really does."

Maggie hollered. She put her hands on either side of Hannah's face. "Oh, my precious baby girl," she said. "Oh, my precious baby girl."

Hannah smiled, not seeming to mind Maggie's hands or her cooing. Their town was filled with college kids, but not a ton of families. People like Maggie knew about Hannah's epilepsy.

They prayed for Hannah. They cheered for Hannah.

They cheered for Wren, too.

But she had to earn their applause on the ice.

IZZY'S LEFT
WITH A MITTEN

Izzy followed the scent of baking cookies to the kitchen, where her mom was straightening mugs on the shelf. "Are the cookies ready?" she asked.

"Almost," said her mom. "But first can you take Row for a walk? Ms. Stallton will be here in ten minutes, and the last thing I need is Row jumping all over my client."

Izzy knelt down and wrapped her arms around Row's furry neck. "You wouldn't jump on any nice ladies would you, Row?"

Row licked Izzy's cheek. They both knew that's exactly what Row would do.

Izzy's parents got Row when Nate was six years old and just learning to play "Row, Row, Row Your Boat" on the piano. It didn't take long for Izzy's parents to realize that letting Nate name their puppy was a big mistake. It was impossible to tell the puppy "No." *No* and *Row*. Whenever Row did something bad like eat a sock, or bark at another dog, or jump on a stranger, and they tried to teach him to stop, Row thought they were calling his name. He would happily wag his tail, hoping for a treat.

Which is why Row was the worst dog in the world. But also the best. Opposites.

Izzy sighed. It was freezing out and the kitchen smelled so good. The last thing she wanted to do was take Row for a walk. But she knew how much the client meeting meant to her mom. So Izzy grabbed Row's leash from the hook in the mudroom and pulled her hat and gloves from the bin where her mom had tucked them away. As Izzy slid her hand into the sleeve of her jacket, she noticed something fluffy and bright pink under the mudroom bench: Phoebe's mitten.

Phoebe must have been in such a rush to escape Izzy's house that she'd dropped it on the way out. Izzy imagined Phoebe searching her bag and pockets, looking for the missing mitten. Phoebe got flustered easily, and it would only be a few seconds before she started turning in circles and screaming for her mom to help her find it.

Except Phoebe wasn't with her mom. She was at Daphne's house for the sleepover.

Izzy squeezed the mitten in her hand. She could toss it in her backpack to return to Phoebe at school on Monday. Or her mom could send Phoebe's mom a text. *Found P's mitten! Want to come back and grab it?* But the mitten, slightly curled from weeks of wear, felt too important to leave for a later time. It felt like an excuse.

Izzy hadn't been to Daphne's house since second grade, when Daphne invited all the girls in their class to a petting zoo birthday party. They'd sat on bales of prickly hay in Daphne's backyard as people wearing jean overalls and red bandanas placed baby ducks, bunnies, and kittens wrapped in fleece blankets into each girl's waiting arms. Izzy could still remember the warm weight of a particular baby duck, so small and soft with its coat of bright yellow fluff. Next to Izzy on her hay bale, Phoebe had held a sleeping gray kitten, its whiskers twitching as if it was having an intense dream. Izzy and Phoebe took turns brushing their foreheads against the animals in each other's laps, murmuring promises that they would love them forever.

Then Daphne, wearing a pink T-shirt with the words *Birthday Girl* spelled out in sequins and a matching ruffled chiffon skirt, had marched over to their hay bale and grabbed the gray kitten from Phoebe's arms.

"Hey," said Phoebe. "I was holding her."

Daphne shrugged. "Now it's my turn. I get to pick a kitten to keep. For my birthday. It's part of the package. So I need to test this one out."

Phoebe had turned to Izzy, her empty arms in the shape of a cradle, tears in her eyes. And Izzy just sat there, helpless, the baby duck squirming in its fleece wrap as if it sensed danger in the air. Even back then,

Daphne had a certain power. It was the baby animals in her backyard, the flounce of her skirt, the rows of goody bags each containing a stuffed animal puppy in its own carrying case. If Daphne wanted the gray kitten that Phoebe loved with her whole heart, Daphne would get it. And there was nothing anyone could do about it.

Izzy and Phoebe spent the rest of the party watching as Daphne held all the kittens, debating which one was the cutest. Every time she walked over to Phoebe's gray kitten, Phoebe's bottom lip trembled and her body curved protectively around the tiny bundle. In the end, Daphne chose a black kitten with white paws that a girl named Serena had been holding for most of the party. Serena was new that year, and quiet. She'd spent most of the party on a bale of hay near the fence talking only to her kitten. When Daphne made her final decision, plucking the kitten from Serena's arms and holding it high in the air, declaring it the cutest of all, Serena's eyes filled with tears. But not a single girl at the party moved to console her.

Daphne named the kitten Snow Stepper. And for the rest of the school year she wore a gold locket with a picture of Snow Stepper on one side and herself on the other side. The locket was long gone, apparently lost in the ocean the summer after second grade, but Izzy assumed Snow Stepper was still alive. Daphne didn't talk about her anymore, and Izzy hadn't been invited to Daphne's house since that birthday party. But now, with Phoebe's bright pink mitten in her hand, Izzy had a reason to go over. To see what it was that Phoebe and Daphne did together that made Phoebe forget the piercing look in Daphne's eyes as she evaluated the gray kitten, examining its worthiness.

"Come on," Izzy said as she led Row out of the house and into the cold. "There's something important we need to return."

Izzy was two blocks from Daphne's house when her heart started to pound. She gripped Row's leash extra tight. Up until that point, Izzy could pretend that she was simply taking Row on a regular afternoon walk. But she'd taken Row on hundreds of walks and she always did the same loop down the block, across the street, along the path to Willoway Pond, then back. She'd never walked the several blocks past the pond to Daphne's street. Until now.

There it was: Daphne's house. Izzy wished she could see inside, but the setting sun reflected off the windows, preventing any view. So Izzy had to imagine what was happening inside. Maybe Daphne and Phoebe were curled up on a fuzzy beanbag, Snow Stepper asleep beside them, painting each other's nails in matching alternating colors. Maybe Phoebe was sharing some secret as she ran a nail polish wand over Daphne's fingernails, leaving behind smooth streaks of turquoise, silver, and pink. Maybe she was telling Daphne the secret that her mom and dad sometimes screamed at each other late at night, but then acted all happy the next morning. Or that she once stole twenty dollars from her mom's wallet and used it to buy candy that she hid under her bed.

The kind of secrets that Phoebe used to tell Izzy.

Then, as Izzy walked up the stone path to Daphne's

front door, she imagined something else—that she'd ring the doorbell and Daphne and Phoebe would invite her inside to hang out.

Ding-dong.

"Oh," said Daphne, opening the door but not stepping outside. "Hey, Izzy."

Phoebe appeared next to Daphne in the doorway. "What are you doing here?"

"You left your mitten at my house," said Izzy. "I thought you'd be looking for it."

"Why?" asked Phoebe. She shook her head as if a mosquito had just flown past.

"Because," said Izzy. But she couldn't figure out what to say next. Because it's cold? Because you left it behind? Because you freak out when things are missing? Because we used to be best friends and that means maybe you'll ask me if I want to come inside, right?

But then Daphne glanced at Phoebe. She reached out to take the pink mitten from Izzy's hand. "Thanks," said Daphne. "It was super nice of you to return the mitten. And that's a super-cute dog. His name is Row, right? Like row the boat?"

Izzy looked down at Row, who for once was sitting calmly at her side. A flash of hope crossed her mind. "Yeah, how'd you know?"

Daphne shrugged. "Phoebe told me. Your brother must have been so adorable."

Phoebe looked down at her bare feet. She stepped one foot on top of the other. Her toenails were painted a deep purple, the polish shiny and new. Izzy looked at Daphne's toes. They matched perfectly.

"Anyway," said Daphne, shivering dramatically. "It's freezing. We're going to go back inside. But thanks again for dropping this off." Daphne added a cheery swing to her voice, but Izzy got the message: it was time for her to leave.

As Izzy walked away, her body hunched against the cold, she no longer wondered what secrets Phoebe was sharing about herself. She wondered what secrets Phoebe was sharing about Izzy.

Izzy hung her jacket in the mudroom and blew her nose, the warm chocolate-scented air of her house lifting her spirits a little. At least there were cookies. But when Izzy walked into the kitchen, she was surprised to see a baking sheet full of crisp overbaked cookies on the kitchen counter. There were crumbs scattered next to it, as if someone had slammed the sheet on the counter, making the cookies jump and crumble, and then walked away. Which made no sense. Izzy's mom never walked away from a mess.

Izzy almost called out, "Mom!" But then she remembered her mom's new client, Ms. Stallton. They were probably upstairs intensely debating something boring like pillow shapes. Yelling would not be appreciated. Still, Izzy was desperate to forget the embarrassment of standing on Daphne's doorstep, in the cold, with the stupid pink mitten in her hand while Daphne and Phoebe's matching purple toes gleamed in front of her. She had to do something other than sit on a red kitchen stool and search for salvageable cookie bits.

Normally when Izzy wanted to get something out

of her head, she would go straight to her butterfly tin of Sharpies. But the house was so quiet, Izzy could get away with going into her parents' office and doing a Draw Sweet on the computer instead.

Draw Sweet was Izzy's favorite YouTube channel. Dori, the teacher, had a kind voice and gave step-by-step instructions for how to draw dancing cupcakes, puppies wearing top hats, narwhals with hearts on their butts, and all kinds of happy things. The food that Dori drew was heaped with whatever made it taste good, like frosting on cakes and ice cream on cones, and her people were always smiling with large bows in their hair and eyes that sparkled.

Sometimes Izzy thought Dori was super cheesy. But that afternoon, she wanted to crawl into Dori's cheery world where bad things never happened and stay there forever. In Draw Sweet land, Izzy would be at Daphne's house picking out nail polish colors and chewing on colorful gummy candy, not standing alone, certain that Daphne and Phoebe were talking about how random it was that she had walked all the way over in the cold to drop off a single mitten. Izzy could practically hear them giggling at her expense.

But when Izzy got to the office, her mom was sitting at the computer. Ms. Stallton had cancelled minutes before she was supposed to arrive. "Something came up," said Izzy's mom. "That's all she said in her text."

"I'm sorry," said Izzy.

"Me, too," said her mom. "I really wanted it to happen."

Izzy leaned over her mom's shoulder and gave her a hug. It felt a little strange. Her mom was usually the one giving hugs while Izzy squirmed away. But her mom's hair smelled like flowers and her cheek was warm and soft. Izzy's body was still cold from the walk, so she stayed pressed against her mom for longer than she'd meant to.

On the computer screen was a picture of Nate's room. Only instead of its normal mess, the room was spotless. The bed was perfectly made and streaks of sunlight fell across an empty floor. "What are those pictures for?" asked Izzy

Her mom closed the screen. "Oh nothing," she said. "I was just fixing the photo layout on my website. How about some of those cookies you wanted?"

"No offense," said Izzy. "But they're pretty burned."

"I know," said her mom, sighing. "This whole day is a mess. Come on, it's Saturday. Let's get out of here and treat ourselves to ice cream before dinner. We need a change of scenery."

As Izzy followed her mom out of the office, some of the relief that she'd been hoping to get from Dori and Draw Sweet passed through her. Someone else was in charge of deciding what to do next. Izzy didn't have to make any decisions.

She wouldn't make everything worse, when all she wanted was to make it better.

GEEZ, WREN

When Wren woke up on Sunday morning, her parents were sitting side by side at the kitchen counter. Her dad read from his open laptop. "Sixteen Westgate Road. Forty-nine Pierce Lane." Her mom scribbled notes.

Wren opened a box of cereal. Her parents startled at the bag's crinkling noise.

"Bird," said her dad. "You okay?"

"Just getting breakfast. What're you guys doing?"

"We're looking for a place to stay," said her dad. "While Hannah's in the hospital."

"You should find a hotel with a pool," said Wren

as she poured Cheerios into a bowl. "Hannah would love that."

Neither of her parents answered. And Wren realized why. Hannah wasn't going to be swimming. She was having surgery on her brain.

Wren was such an idiot.

"We're not looking for hotels, honey," said her mom. "The doctors need to get more information before they operate. Dr. Koffer's nurse said it's usually several days of monitoring in the hospital before the actual surgery. Then Hannah's going to need to stay and recover for several days afterward. I haven't figured out the details, but I think we're going to rent a house near the hospital for at least a week. It'll be helpful to have a home base. If we need to be there longer, then we might move into a hotel."

"Oh," said Wren. "That makes sense. You can make all of Hannah's favorite foods and bring them to the hospital. And by *all*, I mean pasta with butter every single night."

Her mom smiled. But her lips were pressed tight.

"Wren, honey, you're going to need to come with us, too."

"Come with you? To the surgery?"

"To Boston. You can't stay here alone. And it's school vacation next week. You won't miss any classes."

Wren dropped her spoon into the cereal bowl. "I can't leave. I'm doing extra lessons with Nancy all week to get ready for sectionals, remember? I want to stay here. With Dad."

Wren's dad looked down at the keyboard and shook his head. "I'm going to Boston, too, Bird. It's hard timing being the middle of the season and all. But I'm going to Skype with my assistant coaches while they run practice. We all need to prioritize what matters most right now."

Wren couldn't believe it. All of them were going? With sectionals so close?

The only reason she'd slept late was because Sunday was her rest day from training. Otherwise she would have been up early stretching or working on her off-ice ballet at the barre in her bedroom.

Every day mattered. That's why she'd begged for extra sessions with Nancy during school vacation week. She was going to train extra hard and nail her double lutz.

"No," said Wren. "No way. I'm not going. I'll stay with Nora. Or somebody else."

Wren's mom shook her head. "It's too much. Asking for all that help when there's not even school. Having to worry about where you are, who you're with. Please, Wren, don't make this any harder. We'll find a rink in Boston once we know exactly where we're staying. I'll make sure you get your double lutz."

"Yeah, right," said Wren, rolling her eyes. "You're not even a real coach."

Her mom froze, the tip of her pen suspended above her notepad. Maybe she shouldn't have said that, at least not in such an accusing tone. But whatever, it was true. Her mom might memorize technique tips from *Skating Magazine* and watch YouTube videos posted by famous coaches, but she wasn't a figure skater herself.

She didn't understand. Neither of her parents did.

◆ ◆ ◆

After lunch Wren grabbed her skating bag from the mudroom and left. She needed fresh air. She needed to move.

She stomped from stepping-stone to stepping-stone as she made her way along the wooded path that led from her house to Occom Pond. Wren paused to kick a frozen pine cone with the toe of her winter boot. It didn't budge.

When she got to the pond, her friend Nora was sitting on the bench next to the pond's warming hut. Nora stared out at the skaters—the little kids bundled like marshmallows in thick snowsuits, the hockey players hurtling themselves across center ice, the college students holding hands as they flailed around the edges.

Wren considered sitting somewhere else, but the only other option was the cold ground or the crowded warming hut. So Wren sat down next to Nora.

"You missed three major make-out sessions," said Nora. "And I just got here. Like, literally, I just sat down."

Wren shrugged. She pulled off her boots. Only

the thin layer of her tights protected her toes from the cold air.

"And they were full-on make-out sessions," continued Nora. "Not just holding hands. I saw tongue. I think I even saw drool."

"Gross," said Wren.

"I know," said Nora. "Do you think drool freezes at the same temperature as water? Or do you think it's too thick to freeze? Because how majorly insane would it be if you were kissing someone and your drool froze and you got stuck together?"

Wren didn't answer.

"Wren? Did you hear me? I just asked a super-important question. About *kissing*."

"More like a stupid one."

"Geez," said Nora. "Excuse me for trying to have fun. You don't need to be so serious all the time."

Nora was the only girl in Wren's grade who loved skating as much as Wren did. They spent a lot of time together. There were many days that Wren thought Nora was her best friend.

But there were some days that Wren wished Nora would leave her alone.

Today was one of those days.

Wren pulled her skate laces tight, double knotting the ties. She slid her hands into her gloves and zipped her fleece jacket up to her chin. Balancing on her toe picks to protect her blades, Wren walked to the edge of the frozen pond.

She stepped onto the ice.

One stroke. Two.

She inhaled the fresh outdoor air. It was different from the air inside the ice rink. It was tinged with the scent of evergreen trees and dirt.

Wren stretched her fingers in her gloves. The muscles in her legs contracted.

"Hey!" called Nora. "Wren! Wait up!"

Wren glanced over her shoulder. Her blades rocked over a bump in the ice caused by the natural freezing of the pond water. Her body wobbled and Wren slowed. She almost stopped. But then she changed her mind.

She was not in the mood to wait for anyone.

"Geez," called Nora, out of breath. "Can't you just wait up? What's your problem?"

Wren hockey-stopped. Ice shavings shot from her blades like sparks. Nora couldn't stop in time. She glided past Wren and had to turn around.

As Nora skated back, Wren was tempted to tell her everything. About the surgery. The unicorn code name. Renting a house. Even her stupid comment about the swimming pool.

Most of all, Wren wanted to tell Nora how worried she was about the skating practices she'd miss. Hannah's health was more important. Of course it was. But Wren's parents, the doctors and nurses, even the therapy dogs and clowns with rubber noses, they had Hannah covered.

No one was worried about Wren. Not in the same way. Wren had seen the distracted clicking of her mom's pen top when she'd promised to find a rink in Boston.

It was one more thing to add to the very bottom of the list.

But then Nora stepped into a mini footwork section from her program. It was a fast-paced series of three turns that ended in a lunge. Nora loved it. She practiced it all the time.

Nora was the competition. She also wanted to medal at sectionals and qualify for nationals. Nora would probably take Wren's missed lesson times with Nancy.

Part of Nora would be sympathetic. But part of her would be relieved.

And Wren couldn't bear to see it.

"My problem," called Wren when Nora skated past her, "is you."

Nora stopped. "Me?"

Wren almost took it back. But then she saw her mom and dad walking down the path. Hannah was in between them holding their hands, her body bundled in Wren's old purple snowsuit. They paused to talk to their neighbor, Mr. Morris. He bent down and gave Hannah a hug.

They looked so happy. Even as they were ruining everything.

And it made Wren furious.

She turned to Nora. "Yes, *you*," she said. "I'm tired of you following me everywhere. I just want to skate by myself."

"I'm not following you, Wren. For the record, I got to the pond first."

Nora was right. But Wren couldn't admit that. Instead, she turned and skated toward the center of the pond where a group of college students were playing hockey.

Wren stopped at the edge of the game and grabbed a hockey stick that lay in a pile.

Normally hockey players wore helmets and pads. But on Occom Pond, the hockey players barely knew how to skate. So Wren wasn't surprised when one of the players nodded at her. "Want to sub in?" he asked.

"Sure," said Wren.

He nodded at the toe picks on her blades. "Just watch those picks."

Wren had played pickup hockey before, but she had forgotten how heavy the stick was. She removed her thin gloves to get a better grip.

"Game on," said one of the hockey players.

"Bring it," said another.

It was hard to tell which players were on which team, but no one was taking the game seriously. Wren got passed the puck a few times. She was gripping the hockey stick too tight, and her return passes were sloppy.

Still, she was a better skater than anyone else in the game.

And she was determined to prove it.

Wren relaxed her grip. Out of the corner of her eye, Wren saw her dad turn away from Mr. Morris and jog down the path. Every time they came to Occom Pond, Wren's dad said that skaters who played hockey without helmets were idiots who were asking for trouble.

So she was not surprised when he yelled, "Wren! Be careful!"

Puh-lease. These players could hardly stay upright. Nothing was going to happen.

Wren got a pass. She slid the puck to a boy who fell flat on his stomach. The other team took control.

Wren skated backward, her stick on the ice, ready for defense.

Whoosh.

The puck flew past her cheek, close enough that she felt its force through the air. Wren fell back onto the ice, too startled to catch herself.

Her butt hit first.

Then her head.

Pain shot through her entire body, but Wren pushed herself back up. She ignored the offers of help and skated to the bench next to the warming hut.

Her dad was only a few feet away. She could hear the crunch of his steps on the frozen snow. Wren hung her head between her knees, pretending to retie her perfectly secure laces.

Wren fell a lot during practice, her body hitting the ice at all sorts of angles. A knee bruised. A hip banged. A palm scratched.

Wren didn't cry then, and she wouldn't cry now.

She knew how to hold back tears.

IZZY AND THE VIBE

On Sunday evening Izzy sat at her desk drawing. She was just putting the final touches on a stick-figure girl wearing one bright pink mitten who'd tripped and fallen into a puddle of wintery slush when Nate knocked on her bedroom door.

"Yo, Iz," he said. "Family dinner is in ten minutes. Put on a fake happy face."

Izzy flipped the paper over in case Nate stepped into her room. "You're the one that hates family dinner," she said. "Not me."

Nate huffed, a burst of air passing through his

nose. Nate huffed a lot. He huffed when their parents told him to pick his clothes up from the floor, to put down his phone, to wear a hat because it was snowing. The only two things that Nate did not huff about were soccer and his abs. Nate was obsessed with his abs.

"The vibe I'm picking up is that this is one of those serious family dinners," said Nate. "Mom's lighting extra candles. Chances are someone screwed something up. My money's on Dad."

"Why Dad?"

"You'll understand when you're older," said Nate as he stepped into Izzy's room and looked at her sticker door. His eyes rested on a series of smiling cows jumping over moons, as if they proved his point.

Izzy thought about the conversation that she'd overheard yesterday with Phoebe's mom. And now a serious family dinner. *What was going on?*

"Dude," said Nate. "Don't look so freaked out. It's just family dinner."

As Nate left to go into his own room, Izzy turned back to her butterfly tin of Sharpies. She thought about starting a new drawing, maybe something involving nail polish that was actually blood, or possibly poison, but she was too nervous about dinner to think of how to make that work.

Instead, she went downstairs where she found her mom decorating the dining room table with votive candles, evergreen branches, and flowers cut from her favorite hydrangea bush in the front yard. It was February, so the once silky white hydrangea petals were dry and brown. But Izzy's mom had tied the stems together with twine and placed them in a yellow ceramic vase. And suddenly the flowers looked beautiful.

Standing in the doorway out of sight, Izzy was tempted to turn around and go back to her room. Something about seeing her mom adjust the stems so that the petals rested perfectly above the rim of the vase made Izzy even more uneasy.

Izzy's mom always said that it was a gift to be creative and that someday, when Izzy was older and out of school, the world would feel full of opportunity. Izzy could be an illustrator! A painter! A fashion designer! A sculptor! Her mom made the options seem like items in a store. Just walk down the aisle and pick the one that you like best.

But decorating homes was her mom's way of being creative. It was the career that *she* wanted to pull off the shelf. As far as Izzy could tell, her mom was having a really hard time making it happen.

It made Izzy wonder what else her mom was wrong about.

Because Izzy's mom was full of promises. Not just about careers, but about friendship. She promised that someday Izzy would find a group of wonderful friends and that those friends would love her just as she is. They would all take one scoot back and invite her to sit with them on the circle rug. Okay, so her mom didn't say those exact words. But her mom did give that impression, as if she was oblivious to the fact that the circles at school were not expanding; they were getting smaller. And they showed no signs of changing.

What if nothing her mom promised was true? Suddenly Izzy wanted to escape back up to her room.

She turned to walk away, but the floor creaked and her mom looked up from the table.

"Oh, hey, Iz," said her mom. "What do you think?"

Izzy almost told the truth: that the table looked really pretty. Instead, she shrugged. Her mom hugged the napkin that she'd been folding to her chest. Izzy realized that by not answering the question, she was hurting her mom's feelings. But for some reason, it felt worth it.

Row's tail stuck out from underneath the dining table, thumping against the floor in a steady beat. Izzy crawled under to sit with him. With Row's warm body next to her and the dark underside of the wood table above her, Izzy could almost pretend that nothing worrisome was going on. No fancy family dinner, no mysterious ideas, no untrustworthy promises. No drawings hidden in drawers, no beaded bracelets, no lost mittens. She buried her nose in Row's neck, inhaling his scent of dirt and sunshine. When Izzy looked up, two pairs of feet were in front of her—her mom's black ballet flats and her dad's scuffed brown loafers.

The shoes were perfectly parallel, an unnatural

position that told Izzy her parents knew she was under the table and were deciding what to do about it. Then Nate's sneakers joined them, the laces dirty and frayed.

"I don't think we have a choice," said Izzy's mom.

"Afraid not," said her dad.

Nate said nothing, although Izzy heard him huff.

"I think we've got to go in," continued her dad. "Implement the rescue mission."

"Sounds serious," said her mom.

As her parents' feet stepped away from the table, Izzy saw her dad wrap his arm around her mom's waist. She couldn't see their faces, but there was something about the way her mom's hip pressed against her dad's body that made Izzy certain her dad was kissing her mom on the cheek. Izzy smiled into Row's neck.

The next thing Izzy knew, her parents were climbing under the dining room table, wrapping their arms around Izzy and shielding their faces from Row, who was thrilled at the unexpected excitement. Izzy tried to wiggle away, but she couldn't help laughing.

She was annoyed and relieved. Opposites.

"Okay, okay," said Izzy as her dad tried to kiss her on the cheek. "I'm coming out."

"Mission accomplished," said her dad.

"About time," said Nate. "Does nobody else smell that chicken?"

As Izzy's family carried the food from the kitchen and sat down at the table, the silliness that was in the air blew away, replaced by a calm silence. Izzy's mom smoothed the napkin in her lap. Her dad placed his elbows on either side of his plate and pressed his fingers together in a steeple grip. Nate grabbed the serving fork from the plate of chicken, but instead of digging in, he left the fork lingering in the air. Izzy didn't know where to look. Her mom? Her dad? No place felt safe.

"So now is when you finally tell us what's going on," said Nate. "We're not morons."

Izzy wanted to nod, but she was too nervous to move.

Their dad sighed. "Okay," he said. "You're right. We do have some news."

Nate huffed. "Knew it. Bring it on. What is it? Divorce?"

"What?" said their mom. "No one is getting divorced."

"Why would you even joke about that?" said their dad.

"Because we don't know what's going on!" said Izzy. There were tears clinging to the ends of her words, as if they were trying to climb over and drown them.

"Okay, here's the thing," said their mom. "We're going to be moving—"

"What!" interrupted Izzy. "Moving where?"

Every year someone at her school moved. The teachers gave the kid a gift so they'd remember all their old friends. A T-shirt that everyone signed, or a class photo with everyone's initials written on a wooden picture frame. Most kids acted all sad and promised to keep in touch forever, but as soon as the person left they would start talking about how annoying he or she was and how life was so much better without them.

Izzy could imagine all the things Daphne and

Phoebe would say about her. Yesterday's pathetic pink mitten delivery would probably be at the top of the list. A tear slid down Izzy's cheek.

"Not *moving* moving," said Izzy's mom, reaching for Izzy's hand. "We're moving into the apartment over the garage. For a week. It'll be fun. The garage apartment is so cozy."

"Exactly," said her dad. "It's got everything we need. Kitchen, bathroom, sink, shower. We'll throw inflatable mattresses on the floor and plug in some space heaters. You'll be on school break next week anyway. It'll be like camping. Or what's that word I read about . . . glamping? Glamorous camping. What could be better?"

So many things, thought Izzy.

The garage apartment was two empty rooms above the garage at the end of the driveway. There was a tiny kitchen, a bathroom that had a toilet with a chain coming down from the ceiling, and a sink that made angry gurgling noses whenever the faucets were turned on. The plan had been to rent the apartment to college students. Or something. Izzy had never given the plan much thought because the garage apartment had been empty for as long as they'd lived in the house.

"But why can't we stay here?" asked Izzy. "Is it mold?" There was mold in the school gym last year and the teachers said it could make everyone sick. After they closed the gym and removed the mold, Izzy could still sometimes feel the bad stuff entering her body. Even now, just thinking about mold made her lungs all prickly and hot. Or maybe it wasn't her lungs; maybe it was her heart.

"It's not mold, Iz," said her dad. "The house is fine. Better than fine, actually. Mom did such an awesome job decorating it that we put the house on VRBO just to see what would happen. And someone made us an offer right away."

"What's VRBO?" asked Izzy.

"Vacation rental by owner," said her mom. "It's a website where you can list your home for people to rent on their vacations."

"Someone wants to come here for vacation?" asked Izzy. "That doesn't make any sense. There's nothing special to do."

Nate huffed. "Strangers are literally moving into our house and you're worried about whether they're going to have a good time?"

"Listen, Iz," said their dad, ignoring Nate. "I don't know why these people are coming here and I don't care. I only care about us. Renting out your home is a thing that people do sometimes. To make money."

"So we're out of money?" Money confused her. Not the dollars and cents part of money, but whether her family had enough money, or not enough. Whenever Izzy asked, her parents said vague things like, "We have everything we need." Or, "We're very lucky."

But there were other times when she heard her parents talking about loans, second mortgages, and refinancing. Even if they didn't use the exact word *money*, Izzy understood the message—things were tight.

"We're not out of money," said her dad. "But we are short on cash. We have more money going out right now than we do coming in. That happens sometimes. To entrepreneurs."

Izzy's dad was an entrepreneur. Last year he quit

his job working for a big company to start ThinkText, an app that restricted users to one text per hour. No emojis, no abbreviations. Izzy's dad believed it would force people to be more thoughtful, less impulsive. In a world where everyone was bombarded with information, her dad wanted to slow things down and make texting more considerate, like writing letters used to be. The thing her dad hadn't figured out yet was how to make a lot of other people feel the same way.

Nate dropped his fork onto his plate. "This really, really stinks," he said.

Their dad nodded. "Yes. It really, really does."

After dinner Izzy asked if she could use the computer to do a Draw Sweet. She wanted to escape into Dori's pastel-colored world of joy, but there was something else she needed to do first.

Izzy opened Google and typed "vacation rental by owner" into the search bar. She clicked the link for VRBO.com. The words *destination* and *ultimate vacation* and *luxury* floated over a picture of a beach at sunset. In the middle of the screen were four white boxes to enter a destination, arrival date, departure date, and number of guests. Izzy typed "Wellesley" into the destination. She chose tomorrow for the arrival date and the day after for the departure date. In the box for number of guests, Izzy typed "4." Because that was the perfect number for her house. Four people.

A list of homes popped up and right at the top was Izzy's house. It was strange to be both sitting inside her house and looking at it on the website. Her hands trembled as she scrolled down. The first picture showed the outside of her house glowing in the sun. There was the door that her mom had painted bright red, the historical plaque with "1911," and the maple tree where they tied Row's leash to a spike in the ground.

Next were a series of interior pictures. The kitchen with the wood shelves that her dad had installed himself, the stools that her mom found at a yard sale and painted with the leftover red paint from the front door, the living room with Row's favorite napping chair. Then came her parents' room, Nate's room, and

Izzy's own room. She recognized them all. But at the same time, every room looked different than normal. There were vases of flowers in random places, and the beds were neatly made. A navy-blue lamp sat on a normally empty side table, and a cream blanket was folded across a normally bare couch. In Nate's room, the floor was spotless and the soccer trophies on his shelf were lined up like neat little toy soldiers.

Izzy remembered her mom taking these pictures. A few weeks ago, she'd come home from school to find the hallways cluttered with picture frames, patterned pillows, and stacks of books. "I'm taking pictures for my website," her mom had explained. "I need the rooms to look perfect." Izzy had been annoyed to find her desk cleaned off and the butterfly tin moved to her closet. But she'd checked her desk drawer and her drawings were just as she left them. So she hadn't given the pictures much thought.

But now she realized that the pictures weren't only for her mom's interior-design website. They were also for VRBO.

VRBO was what her mom was checking yesterday on the computer.

Renting their home was the idea she was talking about with Phoebe's mom.

And now it was actually happening.

Izzy walked away from the computer. Away from the perfect pictures of her home and Dori's make-believe world of hearts and happiness, up to her bedroom. She was lying on her bed, staring at her stickers, when her mom knocked on the door.

"Izzy, can I come in?"

"Okay," said Izzy.

Her mom stacked the pillows that Izzy had tossed on the floor into a neat pile. She rotated the shade of her lamp so that the seam faced the wall. Then she sat on the edge of Izzy's bed and put her hand on Izzy's leg. There was a blanket between her mom's hand and Izzy's leg, but Izzy felt her mom's fingers wrap around her thigh.

"You know, Iz," said her mom. "It always feels weird to knock on your door."

"Why?"

"I'm just not used to it. I don't think I'll ever be used to it."

"I'm twelve, Mom. Twelve-year-olds are allowed to close their doors."

"That doesn't mean their moms have to like it."

Izzy didn't say anything. The silence felt sad, like something had gone missing underneath Izzy's bed. A teddy bear, or maybe her stuffed lamb. Her mom ran her thumb across Izzy's forehead. Did she feel the tiny bumps that Izzy noticed when she looked in the mirror? Is that why she looked so sad?

Izzy wanted her mom to move her hand and leave it right there. Both. At the same time. Opposites.

"It's a lot to take in, huh?" said her mom.

Izzy shrugged.

"This house stuff is going to be okay, I promise. It's only one week. Then we'll be back like nothing ever happened."

"I know," lied Izzy. It wasn't the idea of moving out for a week that was horrible; it was the idea of someone else moving in. Someone else sleeping in her bed, looking at her sticker door, and sitting at her desk. What if it was a sweaty teenage boy who left his stinky socks in piles, like Nate? Or a nose picker who flicked his dried snot, like Kyle at school?

"Or if there's something else that's bothering you," continued her mom, "you can tell me. I know things aren't the way they used to be with Phoebe."

"Phoebe? Nothing's wrong with Phoebe." Izzy twisted around so that her mom's hand fell off her leg. Of course, on top of everything, her mom had to bring up Phoebe. As if something dramatic happened yesterday, instead of it being one more day in the slow leak of their best friend status shriveling to nothing.

"Okay, good," said her mom. "Because I was worried you were feeling badly about your friendship with her."

"Why would you think that?"

"I don't know, Iz. I don't know what to think about a lot of things these days."

It was an opening, a crack in the door. Izzy could kick the door open and ask her mom what she meant, or leave it closed. Izzy chose closed. She turned away from her mom and hugged a pillow in her arms.

Her mom kissed Izzy on the forehead and stood to leave. "We're coming right back, Iz," she said. "It's not permanent. You know that, right?"

Izzy nodded. But she heard Phoebe's voice in her head. What does that *mean* "not permanent"? That it doesn't matter? That it's no big deal?

Maybe it wasn't a big deal to her parents, but to Izzy moving out of their house was one more thing changing. Her friendship with Phoebe was falling apart and there was nothing to take its place. And now someone else would be living in her house and sleeping in her bed. Izzy looked at her sticker door—the chaotic swirl of animals and objects and colors. Nothing on that door made sense together, but she loved the way it looked.

Real life was the opposite. In real life, things needed to fit together. Cool girls wanted to be friends with other cool girls. Kids wanted to sleep in their own beds.

In real life, things were supposed to make sense.

IZZY IS LATE
TO THE BATTLE

On Friday morning, the last day of school before they moved into the garage apartment, Izzy stood in the kitchen and yelled, "Nate! Nate let's *go*."

"Coming," said Nate as he yawned and ran his hand through his bedhead hair.

"We're going to be late for school," said Izzy.

Izzy was tired, too. It had been five days since their parents told them about the move, and Izzy hadn't been sleeping well. As soon as she closed her eyes, she'd remember one more thing from her room that she needed to hide in the basement or put in the pile to carry over to the garage apartment. But she could still get ready for school on time. Nate, on the other hand, was standing in front of the open refrigerator staring blankly.

"Just pick something and let's go!"

Nate huffed and pulled out a slice of leftover pizza. He folded it in half and held it between his teeth as he grabbed his backpack and the car keys. "Now who's making us late?" he mumbled as he walked out the door.

Normally their mom drove them to school. Ever since starting ThinkText, their dad was rarely home during the week. He was either traveling to meet investors and computer programmers, or stuck in meetings until well after dinner. But their mom was staying home that morning to clean and pack, which meant Nate got to use the car and drop Izzy off on his way to high school. Izzy looked out the car window as Nate drove down the familiar streets of their neighborhood, coming to an abrupt stop at an intersection that had huge holes in two of the four corner lots, empty spaces where old houses had been torn down so they could be replaced with giant new ones. "Why do they knock down houses?" Izzy had asked her mom years ago when they drove past a home that was being torn in half by a bulldozer.

"There's no market for old homes anymore," her mom had said. "People around here want everything shiny and perfect."

"Like a princess castle?"

"Exactly. Everyone in this town wants to look like they live in a fairy tale."

Back then, Izzy thought that made perfect sense. She, too, wanted to live in a princess castle. Visions of sparkling ball gowns and diamond tiaras floated in her mind. Now, though, Izzy wondered about the families who had lived in the bulldozed houses. Why did they move? Where did they go? Was it their choice? Or did they have no other option?

Her parents had promised that they were only renting their house for one week, but what if ThinkText never made any money and her mom never got any clients? Was the next step selling their house? Would her yard be one of those empty holes of dirt someday?

Izzy was about to ask Nate what he thought when Nate put on his blinker and turned from the normal route to school. "Need to make a pit stop," he said. "For coffee."

"Please, Nate," said Izzy. "Not today." School started in five minutes. They did not have time for coffee.

"Today is all we've got, Iz. And today, I need caffeine."

Izzy sighed. The front window of Starbucks was decorated with evergreen trees and smiling snowmen holding hands made of twigs. Large silver snowflakes fell in a random pattern. As she walked through the door, Izzy wondered whose job it was to decorate the huge panes of glass. It was the kind of job she wanted when she was older—to take a fresh marker to an empty pane of glass and create seasonal scenes. Maybe by then she would be just like Dori, drawing only cheery pictures of suns rocking big sunglasses and bunnies hopping among tulips.

The opposite of stick figures falling down sharp-edged mountains and landing in slush puddles.

Izzy stood next to Nate in line. Nate snapped his leather wallet open and shut. Open and shut. He unzipped his coat and ran his hand through his hair.

"Are you okay?" asked Izzy.

"Shh," said Nate. "Be cool." There was only one person in line ahead of them and Nate squinted up at the menu board, like he was trying to decide what he wanted even though he always ordered the same thing.

"Can I help you?" asked the girl behind the register. She had a row of silver hoops going all the way up her left ear. Around her neck was an oval-shaped pearl on a leather string. She'd woven gray yarn around the neck strap of her green Starbucks apron and her name, Simone, was written in thick capital letters on her nametag.

"Yeah, um, hey," said Nate. "Can I get a venti iced latte with an extra shot of espresso?"

Simone took a plastic cup from the stack and began to write Nate's order.

"You forgot the vanilla," said Izzy. Nate always got a venti iced latte with three pumps of vanilla syrup.

"Shut up," said Nate, elbowing Izzy in the side. Then he rolled his eyes and smiled at Simone.

Nate was acting the way Phoebe wished Zach would act around her. The way a lot of boys acted around Daphne. Her brother had a crush.

And by the time he dropped her at school, Izzy was officially late. She had to stop at Ms. Perry's desk and sign the tardy sheet. But the tardy sheet was nothing compared to walking into class. Izzy dreaded opening the classroom door knowing that class had already started. She did not want all those eyes staring up at her, wondering what had happened.

As Izzy pushed open the door to Mr. Blair's English classroom, she wished she could project the story of her morning on her forehead, the way Mr. Blair projected his writing on his beloved SMART Board.

My brother has a crush! It's his fault we're late! Not mine!

Izzy pictured the letters in red marker. Not the crisp Sharpie kind, but something wide and flat like Simone had used on her Starbucks apron. Mr. Blair's markers were always dry and his handwriting was messy, but he never seemed to care. He called his classroom his castle and his students his academic warriors. He expected them to fight their way toward excellence. No matter the cost! No matter how fierce the battle! No matter how challenging the foe! Seriously, that was the way Mr. Blair talked.

"Ah, Izzy," said Mr. Blair as she handed him the late slip.

"Sorry I'm late."

"It happens to the best of warriors. We were just gathering around the hearth of knowledge. Take a seat."

The hearth of knowledge was a black plastic cauldron with a long cord that plugged into the wall. Izzy had seen one just like it at Party City. Mr. Blair kept the cauldron in the center of the room and, when he switched it on, orange streamers blew out like fake flames. When the year started, Izzy thought that Mr. Blair's class, with its special props and flags with inspirational quotes, would be different. Or maybe, that she would be different in it. But she'd been wrong. Mr. Blair may have thought he was teaching in a castle, but it wasn't a magical one. School was still school. And Izzy still had to do all the normal school things, like walk across the room to her normal spot near the bookshelves.

Phoebe and Daphne were on the far side of the room next to Serena and Prithi. Like Phoebe, Serena seemed to have forgotten about Daphne ripping tiny Snow Stepper from her arms and holding the kitten up high like a trophy. Serena wasn't on the lacrosse team, so she didn't wear her hair smoothed back with a navy elastic headband, and she didn't have a stack of beaded bracelets on her wrist, but she was still part of their group. She could do things like fiddle with the side zipper on Prithi's hightops or stick her tongue out at Daphne, and everyone would understand that Serena wasn't judging Prithi's style or teasing Daphne. She was just being herself.

On the other side of the circle Zach, Leo, and Eli

were staring at piece of red gum stuck to the ceiling. In between them, a row of kids sat knee to knee. The only person with space next to them was Otto. He waved Izzy over.

"You're late," said Otto.

Sometimes it was hard to know how to respond to Otto. He said things that could be mean in a confusingly nice way. Like the way he said *late* made Izzy wonder if he was worried that something bad had happened to her.

"Sorry?" she said.

"It's okay," said Otto.

Otto started to tap the floor with his feet. Otto was always moving. His feet. His head. His fingers. He was a tap dancer, and his body behaved like there was music playing in his head all day long.

"Hey, Izzy," whispered Otto. "Think fast. What's one thing that's actually two things?"

Izzy didn't answer. She was trying to look at Phoebe, but also not to look at Phoebe. Izzy was certain that Phoebe knew about her house situation.

Their moms had been texting all week, and Phoebe always stole her mom's phone to play games and take selfies. But whenever Izzy passed Phoebe in the hall, Phoebe only said vague things like, "Hey" and "See ya." Izzy kept hoping that Phoebe would pull her aside somewhere private and ask how she was feeling about having a stranger sleeping in her bed or staring at the sticker door that they'd created together.

Izzy was even up for discussing what it *meant*. But Phoebe either didn't care or didn't want to talk about it. And Izzy was left debating which of those options was worse.

Otto tapped Izzy on the shoulder. "Come on, Izzy," he said. "You've got this. What's one thing that's actually two things?" Otto held up one finger, then two. One, then two. He was wearing his favorite T-shirt. It was black and said "iTap" in large white letters. Izzy had once made the mistake of doodling the shirt in her notebook. When Otto saw it, he asked if she'd draw the same thing on the cover of his own notebook and then sign her name underneath.

Izzy had done it. But only when no one was watching.

"Come on, Izzy," said Otto. "Think!"

"I don't know," said Izzy. Her words were sharp and mean. But Otto didn't seem to notice.

"Fine," said Otto. "I'll tell you. Tap dancing. It's dance and music. Dance *and* music. Cool, right?"

"Cool," said Izzy. She just wanted Otto to stop talking. Daphne had finished whispering something to Serena and was now talking to Phoebe. If Otto would just be quiet, there was a chance that Izzy could hear what Daphne was saying.

Luckily Daphne's loud voice drifted across the classroom. "Eight more hours," said Daphne. "Then it's a whole week of freedom."

"For *you*," said Phoebe. "Theater camp is not freedom."

Daphne shook her head. "I still cannot believe that your mom is making you spend your one week of vacation at theater camp."

"I can," said Phoebe. She looked right at Izzy. Vacation week theater camp had been Izzy's mom's idea. She'd been all excited when Principal Carr had sent an e-mail announcing that Mr. Blair would be running a week-long theater camp that would end with a performance of a scene from *Little Women*. It was the perfect solution to the problem of what to do with Izzy during school vacation week. Nate was signed up for indoor soccer training, and her mom assumed she'd be busy with work. When she'd texted Phoebe's mom and convinced her to sign Phoebe up as well, it seemed that everything had fallen into place. Except for the fact that neither Izzy nor Phoebe had any interest in going.

Mr. Blair leaned over the hearth of knowledge and clicked it on. Over the whirr of the hearth's internal fan, Izzy heard Daphne say, "When is Izzy going to get her own life and leave you alone?"

Phoebe rolled her eyes. "Probably never."

The orange streamers on the hearth wiggled and danced, trapped in their plastic cage. And Izzy's body grew hot with embarrassment, her cheeks flushing. The fire was fake, but it may as well have been real.

WREN AND
THE PILE OF PEAS

Saturday morning. Wren rested her head in her hand. She stared out the car window as her family drove down the highway to Boston.

Her parents had packed the car while Wren was at the rink, and her cheeks were still warm from her intense lesson with Nancy.

Wren had landed ten perfect double lutzes. One. Two. Three. Four . . . She'd done them right in a row, with Nancy clapping her hands after each one and yelling, "Again!"

When Wren reached ten, Nancy placed her hands on

Wren's shoulders and said, "Your body will remember. I'll see you in one week, and we'll do ten in a row again."

Wren wanted to believe Nancy. But she was full of doubt.

She'd spent the past week training harder than ever, ignoring the tender bump on the back of her head from her fall on Occom Pond.

And now she was being forced to leave.

Hannah was sound asleep in her car seat, her favorite stuffed unicorn lying diagonally across her lap. Wren's parents sat in the front seats, each silent and looking straight ahead.

Wren shifted positions. She usually loved this drive. Boston meant seeing the *Nutcracker* ballet at a fancy theater with a domed ceiling accented in gold. It meant flights out of Logan Airport to fun vacations. One year it meant going with her mom to watch the Figure Skating World Championships.

Wren could still remember sitting next to her mom on the hard plastic seats way up in the highest level of the stadium. She remembered looking down at the skaters on the ice and the moment that her mom placed her hand on Wren's cheek and said, "Each skater out there was once a little girl with a big dream, just like you."

Her mom's hand was cold from the soda that she'd been holding, but to Wren it had felt like the warmest of touches.

As her dad changed lanes, Wren pressed her feet against her skating bag. The rest of her stuff was in the trunk. But she wanted to keep her skates close.

She didn't have the Dartmouth College rink. Or Occom Pond. Or Nancy.

But she still had her skates.

"Okay, team," said Wren's dad as he pulled into a driveway. "Home sweet temporary home."

The rental house had a bright red front door and a historical plaque with the numbers "1911." The bare branches of a huge maple tree spread over the front yard. At the end of the driveway was a two-story garage with a matching red door.

It was cute. Homey.

In a movie it would be where the happy family lived.

Wren hated it.

They'd barely parked the car when a woman wearing a cream sweater appeared in the driveway. She smiled and waved, matching the happy vibe of the house.

"Hello!" she said. "Welcome! You must be the family renting our house."

Wren's dad nodded and shook her hand. Wren's mom did the same.

Hannah pushed against the straps of her car seat, trying to get out. Her stuffed unicorn fell to the ground.

Wren did not lean over to pick it up. She sat frozen in the car, her feet pressing against her skating bag.

Moving made it real. Getting out of the car made it real. Even though the drive had taken over two hours, Wren could smell the ice rink on her skating jacket. The muscles in her legs were still tired from her lesson with Nancy.

Once she stepped into the fresh air and stretched her body, all of that would disappear.

"Come on, girls," said Wren's dad as he picked up Hannah's stuffed unicorn and unbuckled her car seat. "Let's go inside and get a tour."

He caught Wren's eye. There was so much fake energy in his gaze that Wren had to look away. But she unbuckled her seat belt and got out of the car.

Wren didn't take a deep breath of the cold February air. She didn't stretch her arms over her head or shake out her legs. But none of that mattered.

The scents and surroundings of her normal life were gone. Instead, there was this long narrow driveway. This cluster of dry bushes. This house that was not her house.

This place was her life for the next week.

She was stuck.

"How old are you?" asked the woman in the cream sweater as she opened the door to the house.

"Twelve," said Wren.

"Twelve! I have a daughter who's twelve! We'll be

in the apartment over the garage for the week you're here. Right at the end of the driveway. Maybe you two could play together sometime?"

Maybe not, thought Wren.

As her family followed the woman into the house and through the first floor, Wren sat on a red kitchen stool. Wren was curious about the house, but she didn't want to give the woman any babyish playdate ideas. Better to stay out of sight.

Finally, the woman and Wren's family gathered back in the kitchen. The woman placed a set of keys and an envelope in the middle of the island. "Please call if you need anything," she said. "My phone number's written on the sheet and I'm only ten seconds away!"

Her hand lingered on the island. Wren could tell by the way she looked at Hannah that she knew about the surgery. The woman had the same look as Maggie, the waitress from Lou's. And Mr. Morris, their neighbor. A thin glaze of hope covering up a deep sadness.

Then, finally, she left.

Wren's dad turned to her mom. "The house is perfect," he said. "This is all going to work out."

Wren's mom waved her hands in front of her face. "I just need a minute," she said as she turned to face the closed refrigerator.

Wren's mom needed a minute all the time.

Wren had once read Hannah a picture book that was supposed to help little kids learn about big numbers. One page showed what ten green peas looked like on a plate. Another page showed what five hundred green peas looked like in a shoebox. The last page showed what ten million green peas would look like in a house, pouring out the doors and windows onto the street.

Her mom's minutes were like those peas.

Add them together and they would fill entire days.

"Take all the time you need," said her dad, lightly squeezing her mom's shoulder. "The girls and I will go explore."

Hannah raised one arm, like she was holding a sword. "Explorers," she yelled as she charged up the stairs.

The second floor was similar to the first, with creaky hardwood floors and crisp white walls. There were colorful touches, like a patterned hallway rug and a shelf under a window stuffed with books.

Wren had wandered into a bathroom when Hannah yelled, "Wren! Come! I'm in the pretty room."

Wren followed the sound of Hannah's voice to a room at the end of the hall. It had two big windows looking over the driveway. Pink pom-poms lined the edges of white curtains. There was a desk with globs of color on its flat surface, as if someone had repeatedly colored off the edge of the page.

But there was no Hannah.

"Hannah? Where are you?"

Hannah loved to play hide-and-seek. So when Wren didn't see her, she peered behind the curtains and looked under the bed.

"Come out, come out wherever you are!" sang Wren. She tried to keep her voice soft and cheery. She didn't want to ruin Hannah's fun, but ever since the seizures began, their mom hated it when Hannah hid.

If their mom thought Hannah was hiding in this new house, she'd come sprinting up the stairs in a full-on panic.

Thankfully, Hannah giggled. The sound came from behind the open bedroom door. Hannah was sitting against the wall, her knees tucked into her chest.

"You found me!" she said. "I was hiding with my friends."

"You're not supposed to hide alone. You know that."

Hannah pointed to the door and smiled. "I'm not alone."

Wren moved the door so there was space for her to sit down. She pulled Hannah onto her lap. The back of the bedroom door was covered with stickers. Hundreds of stickers in all shapes, colors, and sizes. There were ducks wearing rain boots. Hearts in dozens of colors. Even smiling neon skulls.

It looked like someone had shot an entire sticker aisle out of a cannon and they'd all landed sticky side down on the door. Wren was mesmerized.

"Look," said Hannah, pointing toward the bottom corner of the door. "Unicorns."

"Cool," said Wren.

"Do you think they knew I was coming?"

"Maybe."

"Neigh," said Hannah as she ran her tiny finger over the unicorn stickers.

Hannah's hot pink nail polish was almost completely worn off. Wren wished she'd remembered to bring the nail polish bottle from home. But it hadn't even crossed her mind.

"Neigh," repeated Hannah. Then she nodded. "Yep, they knew I was coming. The unicorns say hi."

"Hello, unicorns," said Wren, playing along. "It's nice to meet you."

Hannah leaned against Wren and stuck her thumb in her mouth. Wren wrapped her arms around Hannah's round belly and rested her chin on the top of Hannah's head.

Hannah was so warm. Like a light bulb. Not because she had a fever, but because she was always warm. And giggling. And dreaming of unicorns.

Wren thought about what was going to happen to Hannah on Monday. The wires and the stickers stuck to her scalp. The surgery to follow.

A tear dripped down Wren's cheek. It was the size of a green pea.

There were others right behind it.

Wren pictured the ten million green peas from the book busting through the rental house's windows and doors. If she started to cry, Wren worried that she wouldn't be able to stop.

Wren wiped her cheek.

She refused to drown the house.

"Come on," she said, pushing Hannah up from her lap. "Let's check out the other rooms."

Hannah slipped her hand into Wren's and they turned left out of the bedroom. There was another bedroom of a similar size with green walls and a large collection of gold soccer trophies. Then a bathroom and a third, larger bedroom at the end of the hall with a king-size bed.

Their dad walked out of that bedroom. "What's the verdict?" he asked.

Wren shrugged. "It's okay."

"Did you find a room you like?"

"I like the one with unicorns," said Hannah.

"Unicorns?" said their dad. "This I have to see."

Hannah led their dad back to the room with the sticker door. "Wow," he said, looking at the sticker door. "It sure is pretty. But how about we let Wren have this room. The unicorns can keep her company when you're sleeping at the hospital."

Hannah paused, considering this. "Okay," she said. "Wren likes unicorns, too."

"Wren loves unicorns," said their dad. He winked at Wren and threw Hannah over his shoulder, carrying her out of the room.

Wren sat down on the bed, feeling it out.

The room reminded Wren of Nora's hand-me-down clothes from her two big sisters. "This is *new* new," Nora said whenever she got something from a store. "Not *old* new."

The room was new to Wren, but it was clearly not *new* new.

Wren thought about the girl who lived here. The one her age who was now staying over the garage. She must have pressed all those stickers onto the door and made all those marks on the desk.

Wren walked over to the window by the desk and pressed her forehead against the cold glass pane. If she tilted her head to the right, she could see the windows on the second floor of the garage.

Who was she? wondered Wren. *And what was she doing right now?*

IZZY AND THE
JUDGMENT PAINT

Izzy waited at the top of the stairs in the garage apartment, hugging her knees to her chest. Nate was out "studying" at Starbucks and her dad was at Home Depot buying tools to fix the leak in the garage sink. Her mom had left to welcome the renters.

And it was taking *forever*.

Row sat down next to Izzy and plopped his head on her lap. "Did you see them get out of the car, Row? Did you see that girl? She looked my age. Did you think she was pretty? Prettier than me?"

Izzy scratched Row behind his ear. She didn't want

to be sitting in the garage apartment worrying about who was prettier, her or this new mystery girl. She wanted to be inside her house finding out for herself. But her mom had made Izzy stay behind with Row. So all Izzy knew about the renters was what they looked like. She was relieved there were no boys staying in her house, but she'd spent so long worrying about the boy possibility that she hadn't considered what it would feel like for someone just like her to be renting her house instead.

It mattered that the girl was her age. And pretty. And that she'd kept her gaze on the ground, barely looking around as she walked into the house.

What if she was one of those popular girls who waltzed through life with tons of friends and loads of confidence? What if she thought Izzy's sticker door was babyish? What if her cool girl judgment spread over the walls of Izzy's room like paint?

What if they met, in the driveway or the backyard, and it spread to Izzy herself?

Izzy couldn't just sit there anymore. She stood to find Row's leash. If she took Row for a walk, she'd have to walk down the driveway, past their car. Maybe she'd run into the girl unloading more bags. She'd be able to see if the girl had braces, if her skin was clear, if her ears were pierced. She could look for elastic headbands and beaded bracelets. Not the exact ones that Daphne and Phoebe wore, but something that gave off the same vibe of belonging.

And maybe, if she seemed friendly, Izzy would ask the girl her name.

But as Izzy was about to clip the leash on Row's collar, her mom opened the door at the bottom of the garage stairs.

"So who are they?" asked Izzy.

Her mom paused, and leaned against the wall of the stairway. "They're a really nice family."

"That's all? A nice family? What about that older girl? Is she twelve? Did you ask?"

Izzy's mom nodded but didn't say anything. She walked up the stairs to the apartment and sat down at the folding table that was covered with blue-and-white checkered fabric. Her mom didn't pick up Row's leash or straighten the pages of paper that Izzy had left in a messy pile.

"What?" whispered Izzy.

"That poor family," said her mom.

"They didn't look poor," said Izzy. The older girl had been rolling some kind of fancy bag and the younger girl had been carrying a clean white unicorn with a glittering pink mane.

Izzy's mom shook her head, as if Izzy had disappointed her somehow. "The little girl has epilepsy."

"What's epilepsy?" asked Izzy.

"It's a condition where kids have seizures," said her mom. "It's very scary."

Before Izzy could respond, her dad walked in carrying a plastic bag from Home Depot. "What's scary?" he asked. "What'd I miss? Please tell me I don't need to go back for mouse traps."

"The little girl staying in our house has epilepsy," said Izzy.

Her dad exhaled a long breath. He placed the

plastic bag on the folding table, the hard objects inside hitting against each other with a metallic clang. "Man, I'm sorry to hear that."

"They're checking her into Children's Hospital on Monday," said Izzy's mom. "Apparently there's a surgeon there who's the best in the field. She's going to be admitted for at least a week."

"That stinks," said Izzy.

"It more than stinks, Iz," said her mom.

Izzy's dad walked over and wrapped his arm around Izzy's shoulder. He gave her a gentle squeeze. "Anything we can do?" he asked.

"I told them about theater camp," said her mom. "I'm going to forward them Principal Carr's e-mail in case there's room for Wren to sign up."

"Wren?" asked Izzy. "That's the girl my age?"

Her mom nodded. She smoothed a wrinkle in the checkered fabric covering the table.

"But she's not even from here," said Izzy, shifting out from her dad's grip. "It's makes no sense for her to go to theater camp."

"Come on, Iz," said her mom. "How about a little empathy, huh? That family is dealing with a lot right now. You're old enough to start thinking about other people."

Her mom stood up and pulled her phone from her pocket. She turned to face the window over the sink. Izzy stared at her mom's back, feeling as empty as a blank page. Izzy thought about other people all the time. Sometimes it felt like all she did was think about other people. About Phoebe and how she ditched her. About Daphne, Serena, and Prithi, and how they sucked Phoebe into their friendship like a vacuum. About her dad and how stressed he sometimes looked at the end of the day. About her mom and the client who cancelled at the last minute.

How was Izzy also supposed to think about a girl she'd never met? A girl who looked like the kind of person that Phoebe would love to hang out with at theater camp? The kind of girl who would slide into her very own bedroom and old friendship?

Her mom put down her phone. "I'm going to lie

down for a bit," she said. "Then how about we go to the library."

"Great," said Izzy, under her breath.

Phoebe and Daphne were going ice skating that afternoon before Daphne left for a week-long ski trip. And Izzy was going to the library with her mom. Opposites.

"I could use some help with the sink," said her dad.

He said it kindly. Hopefully. But Izzy shook her head and walked into her sleeping space. She slid the curtain shut.

So much had changed in just an hour. Earlier in the day, when she'd walked into the apartment for the first time, Izzy had been relieved to see that her dad had installed a large piece of plywood to separate her space from Nate's space. Her mom had hung fabric in the place of doors, striped for Nate and polka dots for Izzy. The air mattresses on the floor were made up with comforters and pillows in colorful pillowcases. There was a wood crate in the corner of Izzy's area where her mom had placed her butterfly tin of Sharpies.

Izzy had thought the space was cool, in a glamping kind of way.

But now she looked at the pile of her clothes stacked in the corner and wanted to kick them over. The space wasn't cool; it was small and dark. It smelled like sawdust and wet towels. Izzy imagined that girl, Wren, unpacking her clothes in Izzy's real room, laying out the perfect first-day outfit. She'd probably float into theater camp on a thick, fluffy cloud of popularity.

And Izzy would be stuck watching from the ground, gazing up at what she could never seem to reach.

WREN MINUS TWO

"All right, Bird," said her dad as he stood up in his hockey skates. "It's you and me and the ice. Nothing else matters."

"And about one hundred other people," said Wren. Her dad had found a rink near the rental house with Saturday afternoon public skating. They'd rushed to get there. But so had tons of other people. The ice was crowded.

"Forget about them," said her dad. "Block them out. What do I always tell my players?"

"Grind and grit," said Wren.

"That's right. The two magic G's. You have to work through the daily grind to find your inner grit. That's how the magic happens."

Wren nodded. Her dad's sayings played in her head like a catchy radio song.

Grind and grit.

Head and heart.

Train your brain and your body will follow.

But as Wren took her first strokes, she wanted to tell her dad to wake up and look around. There was no space here for any magic.

The ice was choppy with tracks and dense with people. Some skaters pushed milk crates; others hung on to the boards. Loud music played from a staticky overhead sound system.

"Time to represent," said her dad. He had a proud look on his face, like he was patting himself on the back for sounding young and cool.

Wren didn't want to ruin his mood.

She dodged a dad holding a little kid between his legs.

She veered to the left as two boys pushed off the boards without looking.

She stopped abruptly when a small girl lost her balance and fell right in front of her.

Then she heard a loud voice behind her. "Yikes."

"Wipeout," sang another voice.

"Big-time," said the first voice.

Two girls her age skated by wearing black leggings and tight athletic shirts, stacks of colorful beaded bracelets on their wrists. One of them noticed Wren staring.

"Who's that girl?" Wren heard her ask.

"No idea," answered the other. "And who cares?"

Who cares? thought Wren. *Watch this.*

Wren skated past the bracelet girls. They wobbled as they turned to watch.

Their eyes both fed Wren and made her hungry. She pushed even faster toward center ice.

"Bird," called her dad. "Be careful. This is public skating ice."

Wren nodded. She turned backward into a deep

inside edge. Then she stepped into a layback spin, arms overhead in an open circle, her back deeply arched.

The ceilings lights spun into tight circles.

Wren knew those girls were watching. She exited the spin and smiled right at them.

"Whatever," said one of the girls. "I can do that."

"Really?" asked her friend.

"Of course. It's not that hard. She's just showing off."

The bracelet girl turned backward and tried to find her balance. Her arms wiggled. Her body tilted. But her lips were pressed tight in concentration. She stepped forward on an inside edge and tried to spin.

Wren almost called out for her to stop. Spinning on an inside edge was difficult under the best of circumstances. It was physically impossible the way the girl's body was tilted.

The girl went down. Hard.

"Daphne!" screamed her friend.

Wren stood back as several adults surrounded

Daphne, the fallen girl. She was crying and clutching her wrist.

A man wearing a red skate patrol uniform helped her off the ice. Daphne's friend followed behind. Wren's dad came up next to Wren and put his hands on his waist.

"Poor girl," he said.

"She was showing off," said Wren.

"*She* was the one showing off?"

"Yeah. Didn't you see? That girl had no idea what she was doing."

"Wren," said her dad, "you can tell yourself whatever story you want. But we both know what happened out there."

A tickle of guilt crept into her mind. Maybe it was a little bit her fault.

Or maybe not.

Wren remembered what her dad had said last weekend when she'd landed a double axel. *You make it look like a piece of cake.*

It only looked easy because Wren worked so hard.

Because she trained every day, even when her head throbbed from a hard fall or her legs were exhausted from an earlier workout. It wasn't her fault if people didn't understand that.

Wren skated away and pushed into another layback spin.

Two fewer people on the ice meant more room for her.

That night Wren's family drove into town for dinner. The main street was lined with brightly lit stores and restaurants.

"There it is," said Wren's mom, pointing to a restaurant with funky light fixtures hanging from the ceiling. "That's the place Julie recommended."

"Who's Julie?" asked Wren.

"The woman whose house we're renting. She left us a list of all her favorite places in town."

"That was thoughtful," said Wren's dad.

Wren rolled her eyes.

"Can I get a picture of you girls?" asked Wren's

mom once they were seated at a table. "Just a quick one."

Wren sighed and put her arm around Hannah, posing for the stupid picture. But the flash from the phone reflected off the window behind them and they had to shift over so their mom could try again.

This time Hannah grabbed a breadstick and stuck it up her nose.

"That will not be going on next year's holiday card," said their mom, looking at the image on her phone and laughing. Then she cleared her throat. Put the phone down.

Wren expected her mom to leave the table. To take a minute. Instead, she reached for Wren's hand. "Wren," she said. "We want to talk to you about something."

"It's something good, Bird," said her dad. "Don't look so worried."

"The schools here are closed this week for February break, just like at home," said her mom. "Julie mentioned that there's a theater camp being held at the middle school. It's open to all sixth and seventh graders."

"Yeah," said Wren. "So?"

"Julie's daughter is attending the camp," said Wren's mom. "I thought it might be fun for you. It'll give you something to do during the day. You'll meet some kids your age."

"I don't want to meet kids my age," said Wren. "I don't want to meet anyone here. I just want to skate as much as I can and leave as soon as possible."

Hannah looked down at the breadstick crumbs scattered across the table. Wren didn't want to make Hannah feel bad, but theater camp?

Wren's mom reached for her hand. "I already e-mailed the principal and explained our situation. She responded right away. There's plenty of room in the camp and they'd love to have you."

"No way," said Wren. She wanted to throw something. Or hit someone. But she wasn't little like Hannah. No one would joke about a holiday card picture if Wren poured her glass of water on her mom's head.

Wren looked at her dad. He had to help her.

Instead, he frowned. "I checked online," he said. "That rink we were at is running a hockey camp all week. There's no daytime ice."

"I knew this would happen," said Wren.

Her mom and dad locked eyes. There was an entire silent conversation in their gaze. But it wasn't a conversation about solutions or alternate plans.

Theater camp was the plan. Just like renting the house was the plan.

And there was nothing Wren could do about any of it.

WREN CONTEMPLATES
A CRUNCH

Monday morning. Wren woke to the sound of footsteps on the creaky rental house floors. The sky was still dark, and it took her a moment to remember that Hannah had to be at the hospital early that morning.

But as soon as she remembered, Wren sprang out of bed. She needed to give Hannah one last hug before she left.

Hannah was in the kitchen holding her stuffed unicorn by its pink glittery mane. Their dad sat on a red stool drinking coffee. Their mom stared out the front window, her arms wrapped tight around her body.

"Neigh," said Wren.

"Neigh," said Hannah.

"I'm going to come visit you at the hospital this afternoon," said Wren. "I want to meet all your new unicorn friends."

"Okay," said Hannah. "You can."

Wren's mom came over and kissed Wren on the head. "Thank you," she whispered. "I love you."

"I love you, too," said Wren.

Wren was furious at her parents. For dragging her here. For signing her up for theater camp. For messing up her training.

But on top of her anger, covering it like a thin pair of skating tights, was something else: a desire to lean into her mom's arms and stay there forever.

Instead, Wren hugged Hannah, only letting go when headlights shone through the kitchen window.

"The car's here," said her mom. "Time to go, Hannah."

Wren nodded. She gave Hannah one last squeeze. She petted Hannah's unicorn and kissed it good-bye.

Then she walked upstairs to her new old room and got back into bed.

She couldn't stand to watch Hannah leave.

Traffic. Wren's dad didn't think there'd be this much traffic getting to theater camp.

"I should have taken Julie up on her offer to give you a ride," he said.

"Thanks a lot," said Wren.

"Sorry, Bird. Of course I want to take you on your first day. It's just . . ." He dropped his head to the steering wheel. "I kind of want to body check someone. Just slam someone or something, nice and hard."

"So do it," said Wren.

"I'm too old."

"I can do it for you. Will that help?"

Her dad laughed. "I know you're kidding, Bird. But just so we're clear, the last phone call Mom needs right now is that you got kicked out of theater camp. Or that I got arrested."

"I know," said Wren.

Then her dad winked and said, "But thanks for offering."

They didn't speak for the rest of the ride. Wren looked out the window as they drove past large houses with long paved driveways. She missed the rink, of course. But also the wooded path that led to Occom Pond. Lou's and its cinnamon bun scent. The college kids who threw Frisbees on the main green.

The roads here were crowded, but the sidewalks were empty.

There were too many houses and not enough trees.

And then it got even worse.

They arrived at theater camp.

The middle school was a low brick building, separated from the road by a huge empty parking lot. It was all straight lines and hard surfaces. Wren gave it one last try. "Please, Dad. Please let me come to the hospital with you. I'll sit in a corner and read all day. I won't eat. I won't talk. I won't ask to use your phone. Not even once."

"Bird," said her dad. "I need you to be a team

player this week. And we both know . . ."

"There's no *I* in team," muttered Wren.

"Exactly."

The front door was locked. For a second Wren thought she might be saved. But then her dad pushed a silver button on an intercom and the lock released. A small woman wearing gray sweatpants and a baseball cap popped out of a nearby office.

"Hello there," she said. "You must be Wren and company."

"In the flesh," said her dad.

"Wonderful!" said the woman. "I'm Principal Carr. And like I always tell my students, please don't judge a book by its cover. If you've got to work while everyone else is on vacation, you might as well be comfortable doing it."

Wren's dad laughed, like it was some great joke.

In addition to the sweatpants and baseball hat, Principal Carr was not wearing shoes. Her toes pressed through her thin white cotton socks.

What would happen if I accidentally stepped on them?

wondered Wren. *Would there be a crunching sound? Or would they just squish under my boots?*

Then Principal Carr extended her hand. "It's such a pleasure to have you here for the week, Wren," she said.

Principal Carr's fingers were long and frail, like the lead in refillable pencils. The kind that breaks when you push down too hard.

Crunch, decided Wren. Not squish.

"How about I show Wren to the auditorium?" said Principal Carr, looking at Wren's dad. "And allow you to get on with your day."

There it was. The head tilt. The tight smile. The sympathetic eyes. Of course her mom told Principal Carr all about Hannah. Her mom told everyone about Hannah.

Wren's dad nodded and pulled Wren close. "Love you, Bird," he whispered. "You've got this, right?"

"Yeah," said Wren. "I've got this."

She didn't want him to let go.

Being alone on the ice felt like power and

freedom. Being alone in this unknown school felt like punishment.

Wren pulled away.

"Okay," said her dad. "See you this afternoon."

Wren followed Principal Carr. The hallways were lined with metal lockers and the linoleum floors were gray with a million tiny specks. Lights buzzed in their plastic covers.

"Now, Wren," said Principal Carr. "I hear you're staying at Izzy's house. What a nice girl Izzy is. You two must be good friends already."

Or not, thought Wren.

Yesterday Wren had seen Izzy leave the garage apartment and walk her dog down the driveway. Izzy had paused at the end of the driveway and looked up at the window where Wren was standing.

Instead of waving, Wren ducked.

She had no idea if Izzy saw her.

She wasn't even sure why she ducked. It was a split-second decision. Her body reacted before her brain had time to think the action through.

"Here we are," said Principal Carr, pausing in front of a set of doors. "You're in for a treat, Wren. Mr. Blair is one of our finest teachers, and he's got a real passion for drama. It's going to be a great week."

As Principal Carr pushed open one of the doors, its handle releasing a metal-on-metal click, Wren was tempted to run. Down the hall. Into the parking lot.

And then what? Where would she go next? She had no way to get to the hospital and she didn't even know the rental house address.

Wren was trapped.

IZZY AND THE SUPER-TRAGIC TRAGEDY

From the corner of her eye, Izzy noticed a rectangle of light as the auditorium doors opened. She sank down in her seat and glanced at Phoebe, who had chosen a spot at the far end of Izzy's row. Phoebe's eyes would tell Izzy who was walking in the door: Wren or Daphne. They were the only two people who hadn't been checked off Mr. Blair's attendance list.

If it was Daphne walking through the doors, Phoebe's eyes would flicker with joy. Daphne had broken her wrist ice skating on Saturday and her parents cancelled their ski trip.

"Daphne's super bummed," Phoebe explained that morning when Izzy's mom drove them to theater camp. "But honestly, I'm kind of glad. This week will be so much more fun now. But don't tell Daphne I said that. 'Kay? Promise?"

Izzy promised. And then she'd looked out the car window and thought that having Daphne at theater camp was going to be the opposite of more fun. It was going to be miserable.

If it was Wren walking through the doors, Phoebe's eyes would squint in examination mode. Phoebe had asked Izzy tons of questions about Wren. What did she look like? What was she into? Did she even do theater? But Izzy had no answers. Just yesterday Izzy had seen Wren in the window and waved. And Wren had ducked out of sight.

Izzy's mom had described Wren as quiet and slow to warm up. But Izzy disagreed. A quiet, slow-to-warm-up girl would at least wave back.

The auditorium doors closed. Phoebe turned and squinted. It was Wren.

Izzy sank lower in her seat. She worried that Wren was actually more mean than quiet.

Mr. Blair jumped off the stage where he'd been sitting flipping through pages on his clipboard. "Ah," he said. "A new warrior. Welcome, welcome. You must be Wren. Please join us on the theatrical battlefield."

Wren chose a spot in the back of the auditorium. Izzy glanced at her over the seats. Wren was looking at her lap, her hair hanging loose on either side of her face. When the doors opened again a minute later, Wren didn't move one bit. But Phoebe squealed and clapped her hands. It was Daphne, a blue cast on her left wrist, a stack of beaded bracelets on her right wrist. Next to her was Serena.

"Serena," said Mr. Blair. "To what do we owe the pleasure of your company? I don't see you on my list."

Serena froze. She looked behind her at the closed auditorium doors, as if they might provide an answer. Serena's expression reminded Izzy of Snow Stepper being ripped from Serena's cradled arms, confusion mixed with anger. "My mom signed me up," said

Serena. "She said she signed me up?"

Mr. Blair stuck his pen behind his ear. He flipped a page on his clipboard. "Hmm. Well, fear not. Take a seat and you and I will get this all sorted at break time."

Serena sat next to Daphne and Phoebe. But instead of joining in their conversation, she stared straight ahead, her body stiff, her eyes fixed on the black curtain backdrop.

"Okay then," said Mr. Blair as he walked to the exact center of the stage. "All warriors are now present and accounted for, which means that we can commence with the grand theatrical tradition of the first day icebreaker. And for this morning's festivities, we will be playing two truths and a lie."

Someone behind Izzy groaned, probably Eli or Zach. They groaned about most things. In a row toward the front, Otto bounced happily in his seat. Wren was still way in the back by herself. Other kids were scattered throughout the auditorium in groups of twos and threes, some with their feet pressed against the seat backs in front of them, others with their legs tucked into their chests.

"What was that?" asked Mr. Blair. "Battle cries of excitement? Excellent! Now, the way this works is that I will assign everyone a partner. Please tell your partner two truths and one lie, then your partner will present what they heard to the rest of the group, who will then have to determine what is fact and what is fiction. Are we ready?"

"Ready!" said Otto.

"Wonderful," said Mr. Blair. "Now, for partners may I please have . . ." Mr. Blair paused and drummed on his thighs. Then he started walking up the center aisle, assigning partners from different sections of the auditorium.

Please not Wren, thought Izzy as Mr. Blair stepped closer, calling out name pairs. *Please not Wren.*

"Next I would like Otto and Daphne. Phoebe and Eli. Serena and Zach. And last but not least, Izzy and Wren."

Daphne sighed and threw her head against the back of her seat. Phoebe patted Daphne's shoulder in consolation. Serena leaned over in the opposite direction, as if she was retrieving something from the next seat, but Izzy didn't watch long enough to see what it was. She was too distracted by her pounding heart. *Wren.* She was partners with Wren.

Should she walk to Wren? Or let Wren walk to her? Or maybe they should meet somewhere neutral, like the stage?

Yes, thought Izzy. Neutral would be best. Izzy waited for Otto to tap dance up the aisle toward Daphne, his jazz hands waving. Then she slid between the seats and began to walk, not looking back until she reached the three wide risers that led to the stage.

Wren was a few feet behind, her eyes looking at the floor. Izzy continued up, choosing a spot at the edge of the stage where she could dangle her legs over the side. Wren sat next to her.

"Hi," said Izzy.

"Hey," said Wren.

Izzy was glad she'd chosen that spot. It was better than having to sit facing each other. The decision gave her a boost of confidence. But still, they sat in silence, Wren's feet beating a steady rhythm against the base of the stage.

"I like your leggings," said Izzy.

Wren's leggings were a blue camo pattern, and Izzy really did like them. But mostly she was just looking for something to say. All the other pairs were already talking, sharing their two truths and one lie. When Wren didn't respond, Izzy wished she could take the words back. There were a million more important things she could have said. Like, *Sorry about your little sister.* Or, *Does this feel super weird to you, too?*

But then Wren smiled. "Is that a truth or a lie?"

"A truth," said Izzy.

Wren nodded. "I like your door of stickers."

"Is that a truth or a lie?"

"A truth."

"This is super weird," said Izzy.

"Truth or lie?" asked Wren.

"Do you even need to ask?" said Izzy.

"Not really," said Wren.

They both laughed. It was a laugh that was filled

with so many awkward things—the stage lights shining in their eyes, that they were totally messing up the icebreaker game, that Wren had slept in Izzy's bed the last two nights—so that the laughter grew from a quiet giggle to a full-on explosion.

Mr. Blair looked at them. And so did everyone else.

As Izzy tried to stop laughing, she noticed that Daphne was staring at Wren with a particularly angry look in her eyes. Daphne was usually fake sweet on the outside, especially in front of teachers. But she was glaring right at Wren.

Wren must have noticed, too. "It's sort of my fault that girl broke her wrist," whispered Wren.

"Truth or lie?" asked Izzy, confused.

"Truth," said Wren.

Wren told Izzy about the skating rink and Daphne's fall. Izzy didn't want the story to end. She wasn't happy that Daphne broke her wrist, but she loved being wrapped up in Wren's tale, sitting there on the edge of the stage as part of a pair.

Last year Dr. Forte, the school counselor, had

friendship lunches with the girls in Izzy's class. Every Thursday, Dr. Forte picked ten girls to eat lunch together in her office. They sat in a circle on Dr. Forte's pale green carpet and talked about what it meant to be a good friend, how words can have different meanings depending on how they're said, and how actions that might not seem like a big deal to one person could be hurtful to someone else.

As Dr. Forte chewed on the ends of her tortoiseshell reading glasses and the girls slurped from juice boxes and crunched on chips, they shared stories about times they hadn't been invited to birthday parties or had heard their names whispered from deep inside tight huddles on the playground at recess.

Izzy had been chosen for friendship lunch five times over the school year, and she loved every one of them. Sitting there, kneading a paper napkin between her fingers, the world outside Dr. Forte's office disappeared. Phrases that often swirled in Izzy's own mind—*What did I do wrong? Why don't they like me? Why does it have to be so hard?*—were spoken by other girls.

When the bell rang, signaling the end of lunch period, Izzy often felt dizzy, as if the air inside Dr. Forte's office, with its inspirational posters and potted plants on top of tall metal filing cabinets, was more dense than the rest of the school building. She'd be slow to stand and end up at the back of the line to throw away her trash. But then she'd look up and someone—one time it was Grace, another time it was Serena—would be holding the door open, waiting for her.

As the friendship lunch girls walked back to class, laughing about how if anybody told a fart joke about any one of them the others would totally have her back, Izzy wondered if maybe this was the beginning. Maybe she didn't have to worry so much about Phoebe drifting toward Daphne and leaving her behind. Maybe some girl in friendship lunch would fill the void.

But that hopeful feeling had never lasted very long. Eventually there would be a Monday morning when Izzy learned that she hadn't been invited to a movie or a sleepover. She'd walk through school seeing all the groups that she didn't belong to: the lacrosse team wearing their navy elastic headbands, the orchestra kids practicing to perform at morning assembly, the ballet dancers who'd leave early dismissal slips at Ms. Perry's front desk every Friday in December so they could get to Boston in time to perform in the *Nutcracker*.

At the end of friendship lunch, Dr. Forte loved to say: "Friendships are complicated, girls. Think of them like an ocean wave. They're always changing, rising and falling, but the movement can be beautiful."

One whispered conversation on the edge of the stage didn't count as a friendship. And anyway, if Wren were a wave, Izzy suspected she'd be the really strong kind that can knock you right over.

But as Izzy sat on the auditorium stage scrambling to make up two truths and one lie about Wren, a hard task because they'd been so busy laughing that they'd forgotten the point of the game, she felt a flicker of hope.

Maybe she wouldn't have to spend this week all alone.

WREN'S FIRE

Wren's dad was waiting outside of the school, just like he'd promised. They drove straight to see Hannah.

The hospital was enormous. A maze of hallways and elevators and lobbies. Wren couldn't believe that Hannah was somewhere deep inside.

How would the unicorns possibly find her?

Wren shook her head. Tightened her ponytail. There were no unicorns.

But she desperately wished that there were.

"Almost there," said her dad. He was looking at

the hallway signs and muttering directions to himself. "Just one more elevator and then a left past the cafeteria sign."

"Okay," said Wren, more to herself than to her dad.

"Just remember, Hannah's had a long day. They implanted the wires and she's off her medicine so she's already had a few seizures. Which is good, right? It's all part of the process."

Wren's dad spoke in his coaching voice. With a we-can-do-this pep to his words.

The seizures helped the doctors learn about Hannah's brain. That increased the chances of the surgery being successful. But her dad never looked this tired when he spoke to his hockey team. And when Wren stepped inside Hannah's hospital room, she understood why.

Hannah was asleep. Her head wrapped in white gauze. The same colorful wires that Wren had seen in photos months ago ran down Hannah's cheek. Next to her bed, machines blinked with charts and numbers.

Wren's mom looked up from her chair, her right hand gripping her phone. She stood up and wrapped Wren in a hug.

None of them said a word. But there was an electric hum in the air that made the space feel noisy.

Wren walked over to Hannah and squeezed Hannah's hand. She smelled glue. And a chemical scent. She kissed Hannah's cheek.

When Wren looked back, both her parents were crying.

Wren's mom dabbed her eyes. She wiped her nose with a tissue. "How was theater camp today?" she asked with a forced smile. "Are you hungry? I know I could use some food."

Theater camp felt like a different country, one that Wren could barely remember visiting. And she was not hungry. But she nodded, wanting to get away from the smells and the wires.

As they walked down the hallway, Wren let her mom hold her hand and her dad throw his arm over her shoulder. They moved like a lurching multi-legged creature. Awkward and ambling. But Wren didn't try to wiggle away.

For once, she didn't mind slowing down.

Over dinner in the hospital cafeteria, her parents told Wren that Hannah would be okay.

The doctors were the best in the world.

Someday their stay here would feel like a blip, a hiccup, a long-ago, really tough time.

And Wren tried to believe them.

But something grew inside her.

It started as worry, but it spun into a more familiar feeling.

A restlessness. An ember. A flame.

She needed to skate. Not just to practice her double lutz, but to feel like herself again. Because here, in this cafeteria, in this hospital, in this city, Wren was twitchy and jammed.

Her fire needed air.

By the time Wren and her dad got back to the rental house, it was late. Her dad had to jump on a call with his assistant coaches. Her mom was spending the night with Hannah at the hospital.

Wren went upstairs to Izzy's room. She did three sets of crunches and push-ups. Then she ran through the choreography of her program, the strong electric beats of her music playing in her head.

But Izzy's room was too small. When Wren tried to do even a waltz jump, she crashed into the bed.

So she moved out to the hallway, but it was too narrow. And the rug on the floor provided too much friction.

After spending all day inside the windowless school auditorium and all evening in the car and the hospital, Wren was ready to explode.

She looked out the window, down to the driveway.

It was flat and empty and hard.

Perfect.

Wren zipped up her coat and walked out the back door. She had just landed her third single axel when a dog raced down the driveway and jumped on her, almost knocking Wren over.

Next came Izzy, a leash dangling from her hand. "No, Row!" yelled Izzy.

The dog dropped to the ground and rolled onto his back, his paws scrambling at nothing but the cold night air.

"No, Row!" repeated Izzy. "Bad dog!"

Wren laughed. She scratched the dog's belly. "Is that his name? Noro?"

Izzy smiled. "Just Row. It's a long story. I was taking him out to use the bathroom and he saw you jumping out here. He bolted before I could put on his leash."

"Sorry," said Wren.

"What are you doing anyway?" asked Izzy. "It's freezing. And dark. And . . . freezing."

"Off-ice training," said Wren. "Once I get moving I hardly notice the cold. I've got a really important skating competition in three weeks. So I need to practice however I can. If I were home I'd be skating every day, but here . . ."

Wren looked toward Izzy's house and hoped that

her glance was explanation enough. She was not in the mood to talk about everything the house implied. Hannah's hospital stay. The upcoming surgery. Her parents' worry. Wren's own worry.

Thankfully, Izzy nodded. She knelt down and grabbed Row's collar. "Can you do it again?" she asked. "That jumping thing?"

"Yeah," said Wren.

Nothing compared to being on the ice. But doing jumps on land was better than not practicing at all.

Wren still got to spring and twist. She could give her body that moment of weightlessness that it craved.

Wren took a few mini jumps, then pressed off her bent left leg into a single axel. One-and-a-half turns later, she landed on her right leg, bouncing in place to absorb the impact of her landing.

Izzy let go of Row's collar and clapped.

It was only one clap. Because as soon as Izzy let go, Row bolted.

One second Row was sitting next to Izzy, his tongue hanging lazily out of the side of his mouth, and the next second he was a blur of brown fur running down the driveway toward the street.

"No, Row!" yelled Izzy.

"Come back!" yelled Wren.

Izzy stretched the leash across her forehead, panic in her eyes. She looked back at the garage, then down the driveway to the street, then back at Wren.

Wren made the decision that Izzy could not. "Come on," she said, pulling Izzy's arm. "Let's go."

Together, they ran. Past houses lit from within and underneath streetlights.

They were fast, but Row was faster.

"He's going to the pond," said Izzy, her breath creating tiny puffs of clouds. "It's his favorite place."

"How far?" asked Wren.

"One more block. There's a wood sign that marks a path. He'll turn there."

"Then he'll stop?"

"He better."

Panting, they reached a wooden post. Wren followed Izzy down a path into the woods. The ground was uneven and soft with pine needles. Occasional stones slowed their pace.

It reminded Wren of Occom Pond.

Row sat at the end of the path, lit by moonlight.

He thumped his tail against the dirt as Izzy threw her arms around his neck. "No, Row," said Izzy as she clipped his leash onto his collar and kissed the top of his head. "You're the worst dog in the whole world and I'm never, ever going to forgive you."

Row licked Wren's hand, but Wren barely noticed.

She reached her foot onto the surface of the pond.

It was frozen.

"Does anyone skate here?" asked Wren.

"I'm not sure," said Izzy. "I think I might have gone once, a long time ago."

Once. A long time ago.

So it was possible.

"We should go back," said Izzy.

Wren looked across the pond. Its oval shape. The dense trees beyond. There was an occasional stick frozen into the ice surface, a pebble or two, but it was certainly big enough to skate on. If she planned it right, she might even be able to fit in a double lutz.

Beside her, Izzy began to bounce. She was not wearing a coat.

"Okay," said Wren. "Let's go."

When they got back to Izzy's house, their parents were waiting at the end of the driveway. "Bird," said Wren's dad, wrapping her in his arms. "Thank God."

"I was one second away from calling the police," said Izzy's mom, raising her phone and shaking it side to side.

"What were you thinking?" asked a man who had to be Izzy's dad. He gave Izzy an long kiss on the head.

"Row ran away," explained Izzy. "All the way to Willoway Pond. We had to chase him. It happened so fast."

Wren nodded, her head pressed into her dad's chest. He was wearing his favorite Dartmouth hockey sweatshirt. It was worn and soft. It smelled like home.

But that's not why Wren left her head there. She was thinking about the ice.

And she wanted to stay wrapped in that thought for as long as possible.

"I'm so sorry," said Izzy's mom. "This was the last thing you needed to worry about."

"They're back now," said Wren's dad, hugging her tight. "It's all good."

"So we're still on for tomorrow morning?" asked Izzy's mom.

"Sure thing," said Wren's dad.

After Wren said good-bye to Izzy and walked with her dad into the house, she asked, "On for what?"

"Izzy's older brother is going to drive you guys to theater camp tomorrow morning," said her dad. "That okay?"

Wren nodded. She didn't care about theater camp or how she got there. "There's a pond two blocks away," she blurted out. "It was frozen."

"Was it cleared for skating? Like Occom Pond?"

"I don't know," said Wren. She did know. Occom

Pond had all kinds of signs warning people not to skate unless the ice was marked safe with green flags.

This pond had no signs. No flags. But the ice felt just as solid as Occom Pond. And Izzy seemed to remember skating there.

"Well then," said her dad as he woke his sleeping laptop. "End of discussion."

For now, thought Wren.

She walked upstairs to Izzy's room and threw her jacket on the floor. Her muscles were warm and she placed her foot on Izzy's desk to stretch the back of her legs. But as she brought her chest to her shin, her foot slipped and caught on the handle of a drawer.

The drawer skidded open just a crack.

Wren lowered her foot. She meant to close the drawer, but inside she saw a single piece of paper. It was facedown, but the imprint of colorful marker shone through.

Wren couldn't resist looking.

It was a drawing of two stick figure girls. Each girl had a colorful stack of beaded bracelets on her wrist.

One stick figure girl was holding a bright pink mitten with a word bubble that said: WHAT IF I CATCH HER GROSSNESS? The other stick figure girl said: THEN I'LL DITCH YOU IN A HEARTBEAT.

Wren smiled. She'd never seen stick figures with such attitude.

She almost slid the drawing back in the drawer. But it was odd that there was just one sheet of paper, all alone.

Maybe this page was part of a story and Izzy had left it behind by mistake?

She would give it to Izzy at theater camp tomorrow and find out what those stick figures were talking about.

Wren placed the piece of paper on top of her jacket so she wouldn't forget. As the sassy stick figures came to rest, Wren tingled with something other than dread when she imagined the rest of the week.

A touch of excitement.

IZZY IN PARENTHESIS

"Quick pit stop," said Nate on Tuesday morning as they turned down the street toward Starbucks.

Izzy glanced at Wren, who was sitting next to her in the backseat. "He wants to see a girl," she said.

"What was that?" asked Nate. He turned down the music that was blaring a never-ending guitar medley. "You're in awe of my superior driving skills and my refined taste in caffeine?"

"Not exactly," said Izzy.

Nate turned the music back up. "Sorry," he said, shrugging. "Can't hear you."

Izzy smiled. Izzy was glad that Phoebe was driving separately for the rest of the week. Apparently Phoebe convinced her mom that she deserved every last minute of sleep since it was technically vacation week. And she glad that Nate was driving to theater camp instead of Izzy's mom. Even though Nate was making them stop at Starbucks and they'd probably be late, things were easier with Nate around. If Izzy's mom were driving, she'd be glancing at Izzy and Wren through the rearview mirror, her eyes searching for clues. Were Izzy and Wren talking? Were they becoming friends? Was that a laugh she heard?

When Nate looked in the rearview mirror, it was to yell at a car that was driving too close. And he played the music so loudly that Izzy and Wren could barely talk. After all her recent carpools with Phoebe, feeling like she was always on the verge of saying the wrong thing or not knowing the answer to an impossible question, it was a relief just to sit next to Wren, their bags on the seat between them, and look out the window.

"Arrived," said Nate as he parked in front of

Starbucks. "You guys wait in the car."

"No way," said Izzy. "That's not fair."

Nate huffed. "Fine. Come in. But be cool, okay?"

Izzy and Wren waited by the door while Nate walked up to the counter. He snapped his wallet, open and shut. Open and shut.

"He's got a crush on that girl, Simone," said Izzy. "The one with the gray yarn on her apron and all the earrings. I think she's in college."

"Is he going to talk to her?" asked Wren.

Izzy shook her head. "He just orders, does this smile thing, and leaves."

"Then how do you know he has a crush?"

Because it's obvious, thought Izzy. It's in the way his cheeks flush and he fiddles with his hair. The snapping of his wallet. How he saves all the money he makes from refereeing youth soccer except for the twenty dollars a week that he calls his "crucial coffee fund."

Izzy had done doodles of Nate holding a Starbucks coffee cup with two big red hearts in the place of eyes. But she'd never shown the drawings to him.

Nate's crush wasn't like the crushes at school, where the whole point was to get the other person to know you like them and then deny the crush as soon as that other person found out.

Nate's crush was something that he wanted to keep secret, even from his friends. A few weeks ago, Izzy and Nate had been out for pizza with Nate's friend Tom when Izzy spotted Simone walking with three other girls, all of them carrying bags with the Wellesley College logo. The bags were tan with blue straps and the Wellesley College girls always carried them around town. The bags weren't all that pretty, but the way the girls carried them over their shoulders, stuffed full of laptops and notebooks, made Izzy jealous, and a little worried. Bracelets, headbands, bags. Maybe it never ended?

Nate and Tom had been debating whether the referee from last week's indoor soccer game had it in for them when Izzy elbowed Nate in the side, nodding toward Simone. Nate froze.

"Dude, you good?" asked Tom.

Nate nodded. He began walking again, at a faster

pace. "Totally. Thought I had something in my shoe. My bad."

Izzy was tempted to tell Tom about Simone. To point Simone out with an ooh-la-la tone to her voice. When she didn't, the look of relief in Nate's eyes was worth her silence. Nate was normally the one who looked out for her, especially in public. He let Izzy tag along to get pizza with his friends and sit in the front seat of the car when he picked her up from school.

Even now, telling Wren about Nate's crush, Izzy worried that she was betraying Nate. But Wren was not Tom. Wren was not Phoebe. Wren had popped into Izzy's life and would pop right back out in four more days.

Surprisingly, the thought made Izzy a little sad. But also grateful. Wren was safe.

Mr. Blair made a trumpeting noise with his hands circling his mouth. "Warriors, gather with me on the stage. The time is drawing near for today's theatrical battle. We know the players, we know the location, but do we know how it will all unfold? No! We do not!"

"Do we care?" whispered Wren. "No! We do not!"

Izzy laughed and followed Wren up the risers to the stage. Daphne and Phoebe walked up the opposite risers, with Serena behind them. Daphne held her blue cast and glared at Wren.

Once again, the look made Izzy nervous, but Wren didn't seem to care. They reached the stage and sat down. Wren spread her legs wide and stretched her chest to the floor. Izzy picked at some dirt that was wedged between the wood planks. When Izzy looked up, Phoebe was fiddling with the stack of bracelets on her wrist and staring at her. There was a hint of warning in Phoebe's dark brown eyes.

Izzy wanted to shrug it off, like Wren would. Instead, the opposite happened.

Phoebe's gaze seeped deep into Izzy's body.

"Now, warriors," said Mr. Blair. "Sadly, one week does not give us enough time to perform an entire production. My deepest apologies to the theater gods. What I am handing out now is a scene from the classic novel *Little Women*, which I have taken the liberty of altering to fit the needs of our esteemed group. We will be working on this scene for the remainder of the week. I would like everyone to read it through, then write down on an index card the part that you would most like to play. I can't promise you'll get your first choice. But I will do my best."

Mr. Blair passed out stacks of stapled pages and blank index cards. The first page listed the cast, along with a description of the characters in parenthesis:

Amy March (artistic)

Jo March (spirited)

Meg March (gentle)

Beth March (shy)

Jenny Snow (meddling)

Laurie (friendly)

Mrs. March (nurturing)

Mr. Davis (strict)

Student 1, 2, 3

Townsperson 1, 2, 3

As Izzy looked at the list of names, she wondered what someone would write in parenthesis about her? Creative? Nice? Or would they describe her differently? Loner? Quiet? A part that no one would choose to play.

Izzy began to read. The scene started at the house of the four March sisters. Amy (artistic) is complaining because she doesn't have money to buy pickled limes like all the other girls at school. Her sister Meg (gentle) takes pity on Amy and lends Amy money to buy the limes. When Amy gets to school, Jenny Snow (meddling) tells the teacher Mr. Davis (strict) that Amy is hiding forbidden limes in her desk. Mr. Davis punishes Amy by making Amy throw her precious limes out the window. Then he smacks Amy's hands and tells her to stand in front of the class until recess. When Amy gets home, Mrs. March (nurturing) and Amy's sisters provide comfort and Mrs. March tells Amy that she never has to go back to that school. Jo (spirited) goes to collect Amy's things from Mr. Davis. The scene concludes with Laurie (friendly) and the March sisters gathered together singing and laughing.

Izzy was almost done reading when Otto tapped her on the shoulder. "You should go for Amy," he whispered.

"Why?" asked Izzy.

"Because the script says she's artistic and you're the best artist in our grade. Everyone knows that. You'd be good at playing her."

"Thanks," said Izzy.

Otto nodded. "You're welcome." He drummed his hands against the stage and went back to reading.

The best artist in our grade. There was no art award at the end of year assembly or art team to try out for. They didn't even get letter grades in art, just a simple pass or fail. But Otto wasn't mocking her or trying to make it seem like kids were talking about Izzy behind her back. It was one of his Otto statements that passed from his mind to his lips in one straight line, not the swirls and zigzags that Izzy sometimes felt.

Izzy read the last few sentences and flipped back to the list of characters. She looked down at her blank index card. Pickled limes sounded tangy and gross.

Just thinking about eating one made Izzy shiver. But Amy's lines about wanting to keep up with the girls who brought pickled limes to school made Izzy think of beaded bracelets and lacrosse team headbands, even the matching Wellesley College bags. All the objects that separated those who were part of the group, from those who weren't.

It wasn't just Amy's love of art that Izzy recognized; it was her longing to belong. After a moment of hesitation, Izzy wrote *Amy* in Dori's favorite bubble letters. She added a heart off to the side for good luck.

Halfway through the morning, as Mr. Blair struggled in the dark to get his laptop to play the pickled lime scene from the movie version of *Little Women*, Izzy left the auditorium to use the bathroom. The lights in the hallway were bright, so at first Izzy didn't notice that Daphne and Phoebe were standing next to the pile of bags, Daphne shaking her head, Phoebe with her hands stacked on one popped hip. By the time Izzy saw them, it was too late to turn around. She'd been spotted.

"OMG, Izzy," said Phoebe. "What. Is. This?" Phoebe held a white piece of paper in her hand, her stack of bracelets on her wrist. The paper was worn, not crisp, so it bent in half.

Izzy shook her head, confused.

Phoebe straightened the page, pinching the top and bottom, and shoved it close to Izzy's face. It was one of Izzy's stick figure drawings. She'd drawn it after walking to Daphne's to return Phoebe's pink mitten, but she'd never finished it. She got distracted with a better drawing of a girl with one mitten falling into winter slush.

The last thing Izzy remembered was putting that drawing in her desk drawer. Except she'd moved all her drawings into the garage apartment. Had she left this one by accident? Still, how did Phoebe have it?

Izzy reached for the drawing, but Phoebe moved it away. "How could you do this to me?" said Phoebe.

"I didn't do anything," said Izzy.

"Oh, really?" said Daphne. "So those two girls with the bracelets aren't supposed to be me and Phoebe?

Because I know that's Phoebe's pink mitten and I know you're the one who drew this. And just for the record, I would never ditch Phoebe even if she did catch your grossness. She's one of my best friends ever."

"God, Izzy," said Phoebe, shaking her head. "When did you become such a bully?"

Izzy stepped back, leaning her back against a locker. *A bully?* It was just a drawing. It was her thoughts and feelings on a page. No one was supposed to see them, not ever.

"Where did you find that?" asked Izzy.

Phoebe shrugged. "Wren gave it to us."

"I don't believe you," said Izzy.

"Why wouldn't she?" asked Daphne. "Wren obviously knew it was a drawing of us and she thought we might want it."

"No," said Izzy. Wren barely looked at Phoebe and Daphne, and she certainly never spoke to them. Why would she give them the drawing?

"We could go talk to Mr. Blair about it," said Phoebe. "If you want to. He'd probably love to see this."

Daphne smiled. Then she shook her head. "Don't worry, Izzy. We won't tell anyone. Unlike you, we don't enjoy being mean to other people. But I think I'll keep this. Just in case we need it later." With one wrist in a cast and the other wrist loaded with bracelets, Daphne folded the paper in quarters and slid the drawing into her back pocket.

Together, Daphne and Phoebe returned to the auditorium. Gentle music played through the open doors. Izzy sank down to the hallway floor and dropped her head to her knees. With that piece of paper in her back pocket, Daphne could easily make her into a mean girl.

Izzy (mean).

In her heart, Izzy knew she was the opposite of that. Her drawings were everything she felt but didn't know how to explain, or even who to tell. Was she supposed to keep it all inside? Or be like Dori, drawing cute, cuddly things that only exist in some pretend, pastel world of joy?

A world totally different from the one Izzy actually lived in.

WELCOME TO
PLANET WREN

The *Little Women* scene had been playing for a few minutes before Wren couldn't take it anymore. All those sisters in their bonnets and capes trudging through the snow. She needed to get out of there.

The school hallways were wide and flat, like Izzy's driveway, but better. Less friction. Wren wanted to take off her shoes and do axels in her socks. Or scratch spins. Or anything.

She glanced at Mr. Blair. He was sitting in the front row, flipping through the stack of index cards and writing notes on his clipboard. Izzy and some other kids had already snuck out. He'd never know Wren was gone.

Wren stepped into the hallway and saw Izzy slouched against the lockers. "That movie is so boring," said Wren. "Never go back."

"Did you find one of my drawings?" asked Izzy.

Wren slapped her forehead. She walked toward the pile where everyone threw their bags. "I forgot to give it to you this morning. It's right here."

"No, it's not."

"What?"

"Daphne and Phoebe have it," said Izzy. "They said you gave it to them."

Wren froze. "No way," she said. "I would never give them anything."

Wren picked up her bag. The zipper was open. The drawing that she'd tucked inside the main pocket was missing.

Those girls had gone into her bag and stolen Izzy's drawing.

Wren wanted to pull Izzy from the floor and go find them. But Izzy's bottom lip was trembling.

Her head shaking back and forth.

"They're so mad at me," said Izzy. "They're never going to forget this."

"Why?" asked Wren. "It's just a drawing."

Izzy looked up, her eyes wet with tears. "It's not just a drawing. It's a drawing of them. And now they think I'm a bully and they're going to show the drawing to everyone and use it against me. I know it. It's bad enough that I have no friends; now everyone's actually going to hate me."

"That's not true," said Wren. But even as she said it, she knew that Izzy had a point. Girls like Daphne and Phoebe didn't let insults go forgotten.

"I'm really sorry," said Wren. "I didn't realize. I found the drawing in your desk last night and thought you might be looking for it. I was going to give it to you this morning, but I guess the Nate crush thing distracted me."

Wren smiled, and she really hoped Izzy would, too.

Instead, Izzy stood up. Tears ran down her cheeks.

"This is my life," said Izzy. "You can't steal my room, steal my drawings, and ruin everything. I wish you would just leave me alone forever."

"*I'm* ruining everything?" said Wren. "They're the ones who went into my bag. You're the one who drew the picture. How is it my fault?"

Izzy wiped her cheeks. "Because you're the one who brought the drawing to school." She turned to walk away, down the hallway toward who knows where.

Wren couldn't just let her go. "Hey, Izzy," she called. "Truth or lie?"

Izzy stopped walking, but she didn't answer.

"Okay, truth," said Wren. "Maybe there's a reason you don't have any friends."

The words left Wren's mouth sharp and glistening, like the toe pick of her skate blade aiming for the ice before a jump, its sole purpose to dig deep and lift Wren up.

But it only took an instant for Wren to know what was coming next: a crash landing. A painful thud.

Izzy's shoulders shook. She took a few slow steps, then began to run.

And Wren wished she could take the words back.

Wren sat in the hallway for ten minutes. Twenty

minutes. The red numbers on the clock above the lockers flipped in a steady pace.

And still, no Izzy.

After half an hour, the doors to the auditorium opened and everyone spilled out, heading to their bags for food. Daphne and Phoebe wore triumphant grins. Serena walked a few steps behind them. Zach and Eli tried to trip each other. Then came Otto, the one who was always moving.

That is, until Otto changed course and sat down next to Wren.

"You're new," said Otto.

Wren did not answer. Otto did not take the hint.

He raised one finger to the corner of his mouth. "Not to this planet," he said. "Unless, maybe you are new to this planet." He tilted his head to the side and formed pretend binoculars with his hands, focusing them in a rotating movement. "Interesting. She does not talk. She does not eat. Has she come to take over our realm?"

Wren smiled. She couldn't help it. If anyone was from another planet, it was Otto. It would be an odd planet. But not a mean one. There was too much joy in Otto's voice for meanness.

Otto pushed himself up, his body as rigid as possible. "Snack," he said. "Must get snack. Human beings need food. Will return soon." With his legs swinging in a side-to-side motion, Otto robot-walked to the pile of bags.

Wren's stomach growled. But there was no way she was walking over to get her snack. What if Izzy suddenly returned and saw her standing near Daphne and Phoebe? It was too risky.

Snack in hand, Otto robot-walked back. He sat down in one smooth motion. "Pretzels," he said. "Crunchy human food, good human food. Space invader want to try one?"

Wren smelled salt and yeast. She couldn't resist. "Thanks," she said as she reached her hand into Otto's pretzel bag.

"She speaks our language! It's a galactic miracle!" Otto threw both hands into the air. As his pretzels spilled, Wren laughed, the worry and anger and tension in her body escaping through her mouth.

Otto, no longer a robot, tossed a fresh handful of pretzels into the air like they were confetti. As they fell onto Wren's head and body, she laughed even harder.

Wren wiped the pretzels from her leg. When she looked up, she saw Izzy peering around the corner.

Wren swallowed a pretzel.

She swallowed her laughter.

But it was too late; Izzy disappeared again.

Otto put his pretzel bag down. He pulled on the ends of his lips making an exaggerated clown frown. "Space alien sad?"

A simple question. But in real life, as an actual human being, the answer was complicated. Wren was sad, but with a ton of other emotions as well. Anger, regret, confusion, sadness: they all floated in the hallway like the confetti pretzels.

And Wren didn't want to stick around for them to fall on her head.

"Get a life," she said.

She walked back into the auditorium. All alone.

Just how she wanted to stay for the rest of the week.

IZZY REACHES FOR RED

Nate picked Izzy up from theater camp. Luckily he was in one of his guitar music blaring moods and Izzy didn't have to say anything other than "Hey" and "Okay" for the entire ride home. Nate dropped her at the garage apartment, then reversed down the driveway, off to see Tom, or stare at Simone, or whatever. Nate had tons of options. Izzy had a narrow staircase to climb all by herself.

As she walked up the creaky wooden stairs, Izzy heard Row's paws scrambling across the floor and her mom yell, "No, Row!"

They were sounds Izzy had heard her entire life, as familiar as the dents in her butterfly tin. Izzy climbed a little faster. There was a good chance that she would get to the top of the stairs and find chocolate chip cookies baking in the toaster oven. Maybe her mom would sit with her at the folding table and Izzy would recount everything that had happened that day. And, just like when Izzy was little, her mom would know exactly what to do.

But when Izzy opened the door at the top of the staircase, there were no cookies. The folding table was pushed to the corner and her mom was standing on a chair with her fancy camera in her hands.

"Thank goodness you're home," she said. "Can you grab Row? He keeps ruining my shots and the lighting's perfect right now. I only have a few minutes to get this."

Izzy put her bag on the folding table and told Row to sit. Her mom's camera lens was trained on Izzy's sleeping space, which had been transformed. The polka dot curtain was tied back with a wide navy ribbon, and the air mattress was styled with funky patterned pillows that Izzy recognized from Phoebe's basement. Her butterfly tin was in the center of the overturned wooden crate and a string of twinkle lights looped across the wall right below the ceiling. Below the lights, a dozen Polaroid-style photos of Izzy and Phoebe were taped to the wall with floral washi tape.

"I hope you don't mind that I reprinted some old pictures," said Izzy's mom from behind the camera. "It hit me this morning that I could photograph the garage apartment for my website. I'm going to make a 'glamping chic' section as a way to show my range of styles. Here, look."

Izzy looked into the camera's square screen and a different world emerged. The sunlight pouring across the floor and the pictures on the wall made it look like some cool girl was about to belly flop onto the mattress to text her friends. She'd roll onto her back as she smiled about all the different group chats she had to juggle.

This cool space that her mom had created and the girl who belonged there were the opposite of Izzy. And suddenly, Izzy did not want to tell her mom what had happened at theater camp that afternoon. It was too embarrassing even to share with her mom.

"Looks awesome," said Izzy.

Her mom smiled. "Thanks. It really does. Next up is Nate's space. Wish me luck."

But her mom didn't need luck. She knew exactly how to fix problems. Money troubles? Rent your house. Stuck in an ugly situation? Some new throw pillows might help. Want to attract clients? Win them over with your wide range of cool styles.

And then there was Izzy, who was left peeling pictures of an ex-best friend off the wall, with nothing to put in their place.

That evening Row scratched at the garage apartment door. "No, Row," said Izzy. "We're not doing that again." She stood up from the folding table where she'd been drawing and pulled Row's collar until he collapsed on the floor next to her chair.

Her dad was still at work and her mom was at book

club. Nate hung from a wooden beam doing pull-ups and grunting out numbers. "Five, four, three, two, one. Done." Nate dropped to the floor.

"Do you want a medal?" asked Izzy. "Or a trophy?"

"Dude," said Nate. "Cheer up. And also, respect the biceps." Nate flexed his arm, showing off his muscles.

Izzy rolled her eyes and went back to her Draw Sweet tutorial of a dancing cupcake with a pink hair bow. After the day she'd had, Dori and her smiling objects were all it felt safe to draw. Following along, Izzy wrote, "Hope You Had a Yummy Day" in bubble letters underneath the cupcake.

The drawing was safe, but it was also babyish and stupid. Cupcakes didn't do kick lines or wear hair bows. They didn't have huge eyes with thick eyelashes. Izzy grabbed a black Sharpie from her butterfly tin. She crossed out "Yummy" and wrote "Horrible" instead.

And she felt a tiny bit better. Maybe Daphne and Phoebe had a point? Maybe Izzy was mean?

She was about to start a new drawing when Nate peered over her shoulder. He made a gross *glug glug* sound as he downed a glass of milk. "Interesting," said Nate, wiping his mouth with his forearm. "You've got a dark side, Iz. Never would have guessed it."

"Why? Because you think I'm little and stupid?"

"Hell, no," said Nate. "I think you're little and awesome. At least some of the time. But you're not usually so bummed out. Spill it."

Nate sat down at the folding table with a bowl of Raisin Bran and spooned overflowing loads of cereal into his mouth. Izzy stared at the metal spoon diving in and out of the milk. Did she want to tell Nate what had happened? Not really. But Nate was right; she was so bummed. More than bummed. She was terrified about what was going to happen next.

All afternoon Izzy had been replaying the image of Daphne folding the drawing into quarters and sliding it into her back pocket. Izzy's name wasn't on the drawing. She could always deny making it if she got in trouble with a teacher. But it wasn't only the teachers Izzy was worried about. She was worried about the other kids. Girls like Serena who were totally on Team

Daphne. Boys like Eli and Zach who loved to catch a whisper of someone else's mistake and spread it around school. Even Otto, who was suddenly all friendly with Wren, would probably think she was a bully.

And then there was Wren herself. She would be leaving soon, of course. But Izzy cared what Wren thought about her. Last night, racing to Willoway Pond to catch Row, they'd laughed so hard, a kind of laugh where nothing else mattered in the world. And when they got back to the house and their parents were waiting for them in the driveway, Izzy had felt the same thing as when they'd sat with their legs dangling over the edge of the stage after two truths and a lie: hope that she'd made a new friend.

Izzy hadn't meant to be so mean to Wren. But when Phoebe shoved that drawing in her face, the gray metal of the lockers and the linoleum floors closed in on her, and the only way Izzy could breathe again was to blame someone else for what had happened. Even if it wasn't entirely Wren's fault.

"Come on, Iz," said Nate. "You can tell me."

Izzy hesitated. Nate was in high school, and popular, but he was also her brother. Izzy remembered the chart on his wall where he would get a sticker for every night that he didn't wet the bed, the speech therapist that he had to see for years because he couldn't say his *l*'s, the time he knocked over an entire gallon of milk when he didn't make the sixth-grade travel soccer team. So Izzy spilled it. Then she slid her stack of stick figure drawings out from under her air mattress and spread them on the folding table for Nate to see.

Nate looked through the first few with the spoon gripped between his lips, a serious look in his eyes. Then he dropped the spoon and started to laugh.

"What?" asked Izzy. "What's so funny?"

She almost gathered the drawings back up. But Nate stopped her. "All of it is funny. The hair flips, the attitude. If I saw these stick figures in a dark alley, I'd probably run the other way and start crying for Mom."

Nate turned his chair so that his arms leaned over the back. "Listen, Iz," he continued. "Everything you just said about Phoebe and Wren and whoever else was all about what *they* did to *you*. *They* ditched you. *They* wear matching stuff. *They* didn't invite you inside. You don't have to just take it. If you can send stick figures hurtling down a spiked mountainside, you must have some fight in you. At least these drawings say something."

"They do?"

Nate nodded. "More than a cupcake wearing a hair bow. Keep going. But add in some kind of superhero. He could be devastatingly handsome with ripped abs. You might want to call him Nate. Just a suggestion."

Izzy flipped through her drawings. The turned backs, the eye rolls, all the judgment. Izzy drew those stick figures saying mean things because she didn't want what they represented stuck inside her head.

But what if Nate had a point? What if she reworked the drawings? Added a superhero? Someone to fight back? Would she feel even better?

Izzy picked a red Sharpie from the butterfly tin. Izzy didn't draw with red very often. She used it mostly for flower petals and eyes in the shape of hearts, but it felt like the right color for a superhero cape. The point was crisp, the color strong. But as Izzy brought the Sharpie to a clean piece of paper, she couldn't decide what the superhero should look like.

Not Nate. She was sure about that. But should it be a person? Or maybe an animal? Row could make a great superhero. Izzy could turn his floppy ears into wings and send him flying through the land. Or maybe she should create some kind of masked girl wearing all black with a flowing red cape?

Izzy tapped the Sharpie against the folding table. Row perked up at the noise, thumping his tail as if he might get to go out for a walk. It was around this time last night that Row took off for Willoway Pond. Izzy remembered hesitating, unsure of what to do. Yell for her mom? Chase after Row? But then Wren had pulled her arm with a we've-got-this sparkle in her eye.

Izzy put down the red Sharpie. She picked up a pencil that her mom had left behind. With a light grip, Izzy began to sketch the rectangular shapes of her driveway and house, a few round hydrangea bushes and the large maple tree with its bare branches. She drew Row, his tail wagging, and Wren right behind him, her arms pumping. She placed Row and Wren close to the street, so they were more outlines than detailed people. Then she began to draw herself. But how? From what angle?

Izzy was never great at drawing bodies; that's why she liked the stick figures. But even if Izzy made herself a stick figure, how would she draw her own face? Would she make herself super pretty with long, Draw Sweet lashes and perfectly round eyes? Or would she add the bumps on her forehead and her way-too-thick eyebrows? The last time she'd drawn her own face was for a self-portrait assignment in second grade. Everyone loved her drawing, oohing and aahing over her oval face when most kids drew circles, and the slope of her nose when most drew harsh triangles.

Izzy wanted the oohs and aahs. But she wanted something else: to be proud of what she drew. Not because it looked realistic, but because it reflected the girl she wanted to be.

Someone with friends, who knew what to do next.

WREN'S LONG LIST

The good thing about Wednesday morning was Wren didn't have to get a ride with Izzy. Her dad dropped her off at theater camp on his way to the hospital.

The bad thing was she still had to go to theater camp. She had to see Izzy. And Daphne and Phoebe. And Otto.

The list of people who Wren did not want to spend time with was long.

But as she opened the auditorium doors, her eyes searched for one of them in particular: Izzy. She sat a few rows back from the stage, drawing on the sole of her shoe with a pen. What was she drawing? Hearts? Stars? Arrows dripping blood?

Before Wren could get close enough to tell, the lights in the auditorium switched off and on. Off and on. Mr Blair's voice boomed over the sound system. "Theatrical warriors, please gather on the stage to receive your parts and scripts. We will then embark on a full cast read-through of our very own, very special *Little Women* scene. I don't expect you to memorize your lines, but I do expect you to absorb them. To embody them. To make each and every word count."

Wren had written "Townsperson 3" on her blank index card. She'd figured a character unworthy of a unique name probably had the least amount of lines. She hoped Mr. Blair wasn't going to punish her by giving her an actual part. With an actual name.

The auditorium now fully illuminated, Wren hung back as the other kids walked up the risers and settled across the stage.

Daphne, Phoebe, and Serena wandered off to the left side. Daphne sat slowly, holding her blue cast in the air as she sank down. Phoebe and Serena sat on either side of her.

Zach and Eli walked to center stage. They laid on their backs like dead snow angels.

Izzy sat crisscross on the right side of the stage. Otto crossed one leg over the other, did a full spin, and then plopped down next to her.

Wren let everyone else fill in the gaps while she tried to decide on the right place to sit. She ended up near Izzy. Not close enough that it seemed like she wanted to sit next to Izzy, but not far enough that it seemed like she wanted to sit next to Daphne and Phoebe.

It turned out there was no right place to sit. There was only a least-wrong place.

Mr. Blair stood in the middle of the stage holding a pile of scripts. He cleared his throat and handed the top script to Izzy. "Congratulations to our Amy," he said. "May your love of pickled limes flourish forever."

Izzy smiled and blushed. She put the script in her lap and immediately began to flip through the pages.

Wren smiled, too. But Izzy didn't look in her direction to notice.

Phoebe recrossed her legs. "Pickled limes," she said, puckering her lips and shuddering. "Disgusting."

"Amy just wants the popular girls to like her," said Daphne, loud enough for everyone to hear. "It's the perfect role for Izzy."

Izzy stopped flipping. Her cheeks reddened.

Mr. Blair flicked his head toward Daphne. Daphne dropped her gaze, but she bit her lower lip to hide a smile.

Wren's hands clenched into a fist. She thought of her dad's hockey players and how they sometimes had to be held back from throwing punches during intense games. Wren wasn't going to punch Daphne. But she understood the urge.

Mr. Blair walked over to Daphne, planting his feet firmly in front of her. He held out Daphne's script. "And here we have our shy, humble, sweet Beth. Someone who thinks of others first and herself last. I trust that you will be able to do the part justice, Daphne?" Daphne reached up for the script, but Mr. Blair did not release his grip on the pages until Daphne nodded and whispered, "Yes."

Wren was cast as Townsperson 3. She flipped through her script, pretending to focus on her irrelevant lines about the recent cold spell and the town's supply of fresh bread.

She was actually scanning Izzy's and Daphne's lines. Wren hadn't read the scene when Mr. Blair handed it out yesterday, and she'd snuck out of the movie. She kept hoping that Beth would have to get down on her hands and knees and beg Amy for help. Or advice. Or, best of all, forgiveness.

But the scene ended with all four March sisters sitting around the kitchen table, happy as Laurie sang and a gentle snow fell outside the window.

Daphne begging for anything was as unlikely as craving pickled limes.

Wren wanted to tear the script in half.

Instead, she spent the rest of the day listening to lines about "tender hearts" and "grave countenances."

She rolled her eyes as Mr. Blair encouraged her to "Breathe some life into Townsperson Three's words. Make them soar."

Wren wanted to soar. Just not with words.

By the time her dad pulled into the parking lot at the end of the day, Wren was bursting with energy. She'd been so careful all day. Careful to avoid eye contact with Izzy, to keep her distance from Daphne, to not smile when Otto begged Mr. Blair to end the scene with a tap dance number.

Her body was stiff from the effort. It craved movement.

Wren flung the car door open, buckled her seat belt, and asked, "Can we skip the hospital today? Please. Can you check your phone for a rink?"

"Whoa, Bird," said her dad. "How about a hello?"

"Hello," said Wren in the same flat tone she'd used for Townsperson 3.

"Hello to you, too," said her dad. "How was your day?"

"Dad, quit it. Just answer my question."

He sighed. There was defeat in his exhale and the slow way he shook his head. "Not today, Bird."

"Is Hannah okay?" Wren shifted nervously in

her seat, the seat belt tightening against her chest. She hadn't thought about Hannah all day. What if something happened?

"Hannah's okay," said her dad. "The therapy dogs came today, which was fun. And they're getting some good reads on her brain activity. Looks like they might operate soon. Maybe even tomorrow."

These were all positive things—therapy dogs, seizures that sent signals, even scheduling the brain surgery. Wren shifted to face her dad. "So why can't we try to find a rink?"

"Oh man, Bird. I wish we could. But Mom wants to sleep at the house tonight. She's desperate for a full night's rest and a decent shower. We were planning to have dinner in the cafeteria. Then you and Mom would go back to the house."

Wren looked out the window. She pressed her palms against her thighs.

"Let's just get through today," continued her dad. "Then we'll see if we can find someplace to skate. Maybe on Friday."

He lifted one hand off the steering wheel and held out his pinky finger, expecting Wren to link her pinky in his. Wren kept her hands on her thighs. If Hannah had her surgery tomorrow, there was no way they'd find a rink the day after. And they both knew it.

Pinky promises were weak, just like the fingers they were named after.

After dinner in the hospital cafeteria, as Wren's mom was kissing Hannah good-bye, Hannah had a seizure. Her arms flailed, her legs went rigid. The machines in the corner of her room lit up with electric numbers. A nurse stepped into the room. She gave Wren's family a tight-lipped smile of sympathy.

There was nothing to do but wait it out.

Wren held Hannah's hand. Her mom knelt at the edge of the bed. Her dad stroked Hannah's leg.

Then, almost as quickly as the seizure came, it ended.

And Wren's mom needed a minute.

The result? She just couldn't leave Hannah.

So Wren and her dad walked back to the car, carrying a pile of her mom's dirty laundry. On the ride back to Izzy's house, Wren thought about sectionals. The podium. Her double lutz.

As soon as they got to the house, Wren's dad went into the living room to Skype with his assistant coaches. And Wren saw her chance.

She grabbed her skating bag. It was still right where she'd left it days ago at the mudroom door.

She didn't ask permission to leave. Wren knew what her dad would say, and she did not want to hear the answer.

Slowly, quietly, she opened the back door. After days of following everyone else's plan, Wren was making her own plan.

The air wasn't as cold as the night before, but it felt just as biting.

The first steps were the hardest. The plastic wheels of her skating bag ground against the driveway and Wren worried that Row might hear and come sprinting out again.

That was the last thing Wren needed.

She kept her head down, her shoulders hunched.

When Wren made it to the end of the driveway, she looked back. The lights were on over the garage. Maybe Izzy was somewhere inside practicing her lines? Maybe she was thinking about the drawing? Or Daphne's mean comment that day about her play part?

But there was nothing Wren could do about that.

She turned left at the sidewalk. Through a window she saw her dad talking at his computer screen, his hands clamped behind his head. He would be like that for hours. Wren was free.

As she walked, Wren looked into the windows of other houses. They were full of families doing regular family things.

No one noticed her. No one even *knew* her.

She paused. Maybe she should turn back? But turn back to what? Izzy's room with her door of stickers? Her dad focused only on his computer? Her script crumpled at the bottom of her bag?

No. Wren had to keep going.

Finally Wren saw the wooden post and sign for Willoway Pond. The path. As she stepped from pavement to ground, Wren's confidence returned.

The cold air. The dirt path. The skates in her bag. The fire in her belly. *This* was who Wren was.

Down she walked until the frozen ice spread before her, lit by moonlight. Wren was ready.

With her feet still in her boots, Wren tested the ice. It had been a particularly cold winter and Occom Pond had been frozen since the end of December. But it was a few degrees warmer here, and Wren knew to be extra careful.

She listened for shifting. She felt for any give in the surface.

She heard and felt nothing.

Wren slid off her boots and put on her skates.

The surface was rough, probably not great for her blades.

But once she got moving, none of that mattered.

Wren was finally skating again.

IZZY SEES SWIRLS

Izzy was eating breakfast on Thursday morning when her mom got a text.

"Wren's not going to theater camp today," said Izzy's mom, reading from her phone. "They just scheduled her sister's surgery for this afternoon, and Wren wants to be there." She exhaled. "I hope everything goes okay. Maybe there's something we can do to help. Load up the fridge or leave a lasagna."

Izzy looked down at her bowl of cereal.

"Let me text Phoebe's mom," continued her mom. "I bet she can swing by and pick you up today so I have time to hit the grocery store."

Phoebe. Ugh. Izzy was relieved that Wren wouldn't be at theater camp, but that still left Phoebe and Daphne.

"If Wren's not going, can I skip camp, too?" asked Izzy. "Please."

"No, Iz. You made a commitment."

"You're the one who signed me up," said Izzy. "I didn't even want to do theater camp."

"Come on, Iz. It's the second-to-last day. Aren't you getting costumes today and blocking the scene? Mr. Blair needs his Amy."

"What about his Townsperson Three?"

Her mom didn't respond. They'd read through the script last night. Her mom knew Wren only had a few lines, and it was obvious that Mr. Blair had added them just so there would be enough parts for everyone.

Someone else might have been disappointed. But yesterday Wren had read her lines as if she couldn't have cared less. And even though Izzy had initially been excited to get the part of Amy, it didn't last long. Daphne's comment about Izzy just wanting to be popular had cut through Izzy like a knife, slicing away her pride at being cast as both an artist and the lead role. Then Wren had read her lines like a monotone zombie, reminding everyone of just how pointless theater camp was in the first place.

When they did a second read-through, a lot of kids followed Wren's lead, their performances getting worse and worse. Daphne and Phoebe seemed to mess up their lines on purpose, laughing like it was a hilarious coincidence. Eli, who was playing Mr. Davis, spoke with such fake exaggerated anger that his spit globs landed on Izzy's cheek. Only Otto seemed to be trying hard, mostly because he'd convinced Mr. Blair to let him do a tap routine for the grand finale instead of singing.

"Please, Mom," said Izzy. "It's just theater camp. It's so stupid."

"That attitude is going to get you nowhere, Iz. And please stop whining. You're way too old for it."

Izzy dumped her bowl of cereal into the sink even though it was half full and the soggy Cheerios would clog the drain. "I'm old enough to decide that I'm. Not. Going."

As soon as the words left her mouth, Izzy realized that she didn't stand a chance of getting her way. Sometimes it felt like twelve wasn't even a real age, but more of a joke.

Too old to stomp your feet and whine. Too young to actually decide anything important.

Mr. Blair had raided the costume closet and found a cardboard box full of bonnets and cloaks. Izzy stood in the hallway with Phoebe, Daphne, and Serena sorting through the pile. The wrinkled costumes smelled like mothballs.

"Here," said Phoebe, pinching a white bonnet patterned with tiny rosebuds between her fingers and passing it to Daphne. "This would be great for you, Beth."

"Ugh," said Daphne. "I hate being Beth. She's such a loser scaredy-cat."

"Not really," said Serena, who was playing Mrs. March.

Daphne froze, her hand with the stack of bracelets

gripping the bonnet. "Yes, she is. She doesn't even go to regular school."

Serena looked down at her shoes. "Beth is scared of things. But it's because she cares about everyone and really watches over them, you know? She doesn't want anything bad to happen to her family."

Yes, thought Izzy. *You're right*. Even though Daphne was doing a terrible job playing Beth, it was obvious from the written lines how much Beth loved her family. But Izzy didn't say anything. As far as Izzy knew, neither Daphne nor Phoebe had mentioned the drawing to Serena, or anyone else. Maybe they'd forgotten about it, or maybe they were waiting for the right moment. Either way, it was safest to stay quiet and not risk finding out.

"She also doesn't want anything bad to happen to Laurie!" said Otto. He jumped out from behind a row of lockers, wearing a top hat and a velvet coat with brass buttons. He bowed, unfurled his arms in tight circles, and did a fast tap dance move with his feet. "At your service."

"Whatever," said Daphne. She tried to tie the

bonnet under her chin and accidentally hit herself in the face with her cast. She threw the bonnet to the ground. "This is so annoying. Let's talk about something way more important."

"Like the epic sleepover Saturday night?" said Phoebe.

"Yep," said Daphne. "I went to the mall and made these."

Daphne walked over to her bag and pulled out four blue envelopes, almost the exact color of Izzy's techno blue Sharpie. The envelopes were sealed shut, but there was something bulky inside that made them wrinkle. Daphne handed one to Phoebe and, after hesitating for a second, one to Serena. There was a third envelope in her hand.

Izzy knew the envelope wasn't for her, but she couldn't help hoping that it was.

"Can I open it now?" asked Phoebe. She held the envelope in her palms, like it was a delicate robin's egg.

"Sure," said Daphne. "Go for it."

Phoebe carefully slid her finger under the seal. It

was not how Phoebe normally did things. She wasn't the person who made a careful slit in a pack of Skittles and gently poured the candy into her open palm. Phoebe was the person who tore the pack open so fast that Skittles exploded into the air. But with this envelope, Phoebe was slow. And gentle. She reached her hand inside and pulled out a beaded bracelet.

Another matching bracelet. Izzy would have turned away, but the bracelet was different from any other beaded bracelet that Izzy had ever seen. The beads looked tie-dyed in bright colors—fuchsia, tangerine, violet—all swirled together on each individual bead.

"OMG," said Phoebe, sliding it onto her wrist. "It's an ultra rare. With real stones."

"Of course," said Daphne. She held out her wrist, where the exact same bracelet rested on top of her stack.

"So this is my ticket?" asked Phoebe. She pulled out a techno blue piece of paper from the envelope and held it far enough away that Izzy could easily read every word.

Congrats!

You've been invited to Daphne's Epic Sleepover on Saturday night!

Only people with this exact bracelet will be allowed to enter!

Absolutely Positively No Exceptions!

See you then!

XOXO Daphne

"Yep," said Daphne. "No one can get into the sleepover without one."

Serena examined her identical tie-dye bracelet, then slid it on. Daphne walked toward Izzy, the third envelope in her hand..

And Izzy couldn't help it. Her heart beat faster. It made no sense that Daphne would give her a bracelet.

It was the opposite of what should happen. But that didn't stop Izzy from desperately wishing it would.

Daphne held out the techno blue envelope to Izzy. "Hey, Izzy," said Daphne. "Since Wren's not here would you mind giving this to her? Tell her to open it ASAP."

As Izzy held the envelope in her hand, she noticed Wren's name written in capital letters.

The envelope was never meant for her.

That afternoon, Izzy did a horrible job in the dress rehearsal of their scene. She was supposed to be heartbroken to throw away her pickled limes, but she could barely remember how many limes she was supposed to throw, or where she was supposed to throw them.

Why? Why would Daphne invite Wren to the sleepover?

It was all Izzy could think about. Finally the rehearsal ended. Izzy was stuffing her cloak back into the cardboard box when Otto appeared. "She's trying to make you upset."

"Who?" asked Izzy.

"Daphne. She's trying to make you angry."

"How do you know?"

"Because," said Otto. "It's her specialty. Everybody has one thing they're really good at. Mine is tap dancing; yours is drawing. And Daphne's is making other people feel bad. She's the queen of mean." Otto crossed one foot in front of the other, did a full turn, and shook his hands as if to say, Ta-da!

"It's not the same thing," said Izzy. She agreed with the general idea, but being mean wasn't a specialty. It was just who Daphne was.

"Why not?" asked Otto. "She practices all the time and she's really good at it. I don't see the difference."

Otto had obviously been thinking about this. Kids at school mimicked Otto behind his back. They followed him down the hallway doing exaggerated tap dance moves. But Otto always ignored them. He tacked flyers about his tap dancing recitals on the bulletin board next to the library and handed out personal invitations to his favorite teachers with a big smile and a firm handshake. So Izzy assumed that he didn't care. But maybe he did, more than he let on.

"If you let her bother you, she'll win," said Otto. "Then you'll be just like everyone else. Congratulations. Victory to Daphne!"

Otto walked off, shaking an imaginary trophy in his hands, Daphne's name echoing in Izzy's ears.

MAKE THEM PROUD, WREN

Hannah's surgery was a success.

Wren's mom was so relieved that she agreed to switch places with Wren's dad. He would spend the night in the hospital, and she would go back to the house with Wren to sleep in a real bed.

They would order pizza and watch a movie. Or at least some puppy videos on YouTube.

But as soon as they got back to rental house, Wren's mom laid down on the couch. Within seconds, she fell asleep.

Wren placed a blanket over her mom, folding it

under her chin. Then Wren did something she hadn't done in a long time: she kissed her mom's cheek.

For years, kissing her mom made Wren feel babyish. Immature.

But that evening, when her lips pressed against her mom's cheek, Wren felt older. And responsible.

She checked the time. Six o'clock. She could skate for an hour and still be back in time to warm the lasagna that Izzy's mom had left by the back door with cooking instructions taped to the top.

Wren would wake her mom to a fully prepared dinner. Her mom would be so happy. And proud.

Over dinner Wren could tell her mom about Daphne and the debacle with Izzy's drawing. Or they could talk about next week. What Wren needed to focus on in preparation for sectionals.

But first, she was going out to skate.

Wren closed the back door behind her. She rolled her skating bag down the sidewalk. There were more cars on the street than last night and headlights shone in her eyes.

Maybe one of the kids from theater camp would drive by and see her walking in the dark. Maybe they'd wonder where she was going.

But no one would pull over to ask.

Well, Otto might. Even after Wren told him to get a life, he still smiled and clapped silently after she spoke her pathetic play lines.

But no one else would. Not even Izzy. She'd barely looked at Wren since the horrible thing Wren said in the hallway.

Wren reached the Willoway Pond sign. She turned down the path. The moon was not as bright as the night before and Wren stumbled on a tree root. Her skating bag slammed against her leg.

But she made it to the end of the path. The low moon cleared the treetops and shone on the pond. And the entire world lightened.

Wren laced her skates and balanced on her toe picks as she stepped onto the frozen surface.

She took a few slow strokes, her legs adjusting from the forward motion of walking to the sideways sliding of her pushes against the ice.

When she'd skated last night, Wren didn't try to jump. The surface was too uneven, and she wasn't sure how thick the ice was. It had been enough just to stroke and spin.

But now, Wren couldn't resist. Hannah's surgery was over. She'd be going home with her dad in two days.

Home to the ice rink. To Nancy. To Nora. And all the other girls she'd be competing against at sectionals in just over two weeks.

Wren turned backward.

She would start with a toe loop. A simple half turn rotation that was part of her warm-up routine. If that went well, she'd move on.

To salchows and axels and maybe, just maybe, a double lutz.

Wren reached her left toe pick into the ice.

It dug deeper than she'd expected.

Wren hockey-stopped. Looked down.

The crack ran from the entry point of her toe pick to a few feet away.

She froze.

Groan. Groooaaan.

More cracks. The lines were delicate. Alive. They spread like branches on a tree, growing outward from a central base.

Wren's heart beat was so strong in her chest that she wondered if its vibration was making the ice shift. Because otherwise, her body was as still as it could possibly be.

She was terrified to move.

Wren thought about the Polar Bear Plunge at the Dartmouth Winter Carnival. The college kids carved a circular hole in the ice at Occom Pond and stripped down to their bathing suits to jump in. They wrapped ropes around their waists before jumping, and someone on firm land held on to the other end. When Wren had asked her dad why the jumpers needed the ropes, he explained that falling into water that cold can shock the system and cause someone's heart to stop beating. The rope was to pull people up in case that happens.

"It's the definition of youthful stupidity," her dad

had continued as a girl in a bikini jumped into the hole. "Flirting with death for fun. She must be from California."

"Why California?" Wren had asked.

"Because no one from New Hampshire would ever be that stupid."

That was the worst part.

Wren had known skating on an unmarked pond was stupid.

But she'd done it anyway. With no rope. No one waiting on firm land.

IZZY LEAPS

Izzy lay on her air mattress, the techno blue envelope with Wren's name resting on her stomach. She ran one corner of the envelope under her fingernail. Then she flicked the envelope toward the ceiling, hoping it would float through the air like a feather. Instead, it landed smack on Izzy's face. If she threw the envelope in the trash underneath the kitchen sink, it would probably still find its way back to her.

There was only one way to get rid of this thing: Izzy had to give it to Wren.

If you let her bother you, she'll win. That's what Otto had said.

Wren would be gone in two days, but Daphne wasn't going anywhere. Izzy did not want to let her win.

Izzy walked into the kitchen area where her mom was making a salad. "Can I go see if Wren's back from the hospital?" she asked. "To check how she's doing?"

Her mom smiled. "That's a wonderful idea, Iz. Want me to come with you? I want to make sure they saw the instructions for the lasagna."

"It's okay," said Izzy. "I'll ask."

"Just come back soon. Dinner's in ten minutes."

The driveway stretched before her, as if it had somehow gotten longer. Izzy hoped Wren's dad would answer the door. Izzy wanted to hand off the envelope and run back to the garage apartment. She did not want to talk to Wren.

Ding-dong.

It was strange to ring the back doorbell to her own house knowing that her family wasn't inside, that

Row's scampering feet would not be charging across the hardwood floors.

Ding-dong. Ding-dong.

Izzy was about to walk to the front door and slide the envelope through the brass mail slot when Wren's mom appeared. Izzy hadn't seen her since the day Wren's family arrived, and was surprised by how tired she looked.

"Can I help you?" asked Wren's mom. She kept the door half closed, as if Izzy was a kid selling cookies for a school fundraiser.

"Is Wren home? I have something for her."

"Something for Wren?"

"From theater camp today."

Wren's mom raised her hand to her forehead. "Oh, you must be Izzy. Of course. Come in, please. Wren's inside."

Izzy stepped into the house. *Her house.* So many things were different. The teakettle was on the wrong half of the stove, the red stools were covered with crumbs, and wrinkled hand towels were shoved in a corner of the counter.

"I know it's a mess," said Wren's mom. "The whole week has been a whirlwind. I promise we'll clean everything up before we leave. Let me just get Wren." She walked toward the stairs to the second floor. "Wren! Wren! Izzy's here to see you!"

They waited ten seconds. Thirty seconds. Wren was obviously ignoring them.

"It's okay," said Izzy. "I just wanted to give this to Wren. I don't need to talk to her." Izzy tried to hand the envelope to Wren's mom, but she had started walking up the stairs.

"It's just . . . I know she's here somewhere," said Wren's mom. "Where else would she be? Come on, let's check her room."

You mean my room, thought Izzy as she followed, the wooden stairway railing so familiar in her hand. They walked down the hallway with the clean white walls, past Nate's room with its row of soccer trophies, and into her own room. The bed was made and the desk clean. A pile of Wren's clothes was folded on top of the dresser.

Deep inside, under all the hurt and confusion, Izzy

was grateful that at least Wren had taken good care of her room.

Wren's mom turned in a circle. She opened the closet door. She patted the pockets of her jeans, as if she was feeling for her phone. "Oh my God, Wren! Wren! Where is she? Did she go out? She doesn't know anyone here. Does she?"

Izzy gripped the envelope in her hand. Had Wren actually had become friends with Daphne and Phoebe? Had Wren actually given them the drawing? Had they bonded in the school bathroom, or hung out after theater camp yesterday without Izzy knowing? It was highly unlikely, but possible. And it would explain the invitation with Wren's name on it. Daphne and Phoebe knew Wren was renting Izzy's house. Maybe they'd stopped by and told Wren about the epic sleepover in person? Maybe Wren had gone to one of their houses to hang out?

"I'll go get my mom," said Izzy. "She has a school directory. Maybe she can call around."

Wren's mom sat down on Izzy's bed, nodded, and started to sob.

Izzy barely noticed the pounding of her legs or the cold against her cheeks as she ran through her house, down the driveway, and up to the garage apartment. It was only when Row jumped on her, his paws digging into her thighs, that Izzy realized how fast she'd sprinted up the stairs. "Mom, Wren's missing!"

"Missing?"

"Her mom doesn't know where she is. She's not at the house. Maybe she went to Daphne's house. Or Phoebe's. Can you help?"

"Of course. I'll come right over."

Izzy waited by the door as her mom put on a sweater and grabbed her phone. She almost left the techno blue envelope in the garage apartment, but at the last minute she shoved it in the front pocket of her coat. Then she ran back to the house with her mom, standing at the kitchen island as her mom texted Phoebe's mom and tried to remember the password for the school directory to find Daphne's information.

Wren's mom paced from the kitchen to the mudroom and back. She froze. "Wren's skating bag.

Where is it? I could've sworn I saw it here."

Izzy looked out the window to the driveway where she'd found Wren jumping in place in the freezing night air. She remembered Wren's question about Willoway Pond—*Does anyone skate here?*

"Mom," said Izzy.

"Hold on, Iz. I need to concentrate."

But Izzy couldn't wait. She zipped her coat all the way up and went for the back door. "Wren might have gone to Willoway Pond. I can go check."

"The pond at night? No way."

"Please, Mom," said Izzy. "I'll be right back."

Izzy's mom brought the top of her phone to her lips. She looked at Wren's mom, who stood with her hands interlaced at her chin.

"Okay," said Izzy's mom. "Go check. But come right back."

WREN AND
THE ANGRY ICE

Exhausted from standing, Wren lowered her body to the ice.

She reached for the slippery surface with tented fingers, an attempt to ease the transition and distribute her weight. To keep the ice happy.

The ice was not happy. Its cracks splintered and grew.

But it held. For now.

Wren wasn't wearing a watch and didn't have a phone. Based on the stiffness in her fingers and the numbness of her toes, she'd probably been stuck for at least an hour. Her mom might wake up soon. Maybe she'd call Wren's name and realize she wasn't home.

Or maybe not.

And that was only half the problem.

The other half was that no one knew where she was.

Wren tried to scream. *"Help!"* But her tired voice refused to cooperate.

She could see houses through the tree branches, but they were faraway. Their windows shut. Their doors closed. Keeping out the cold.

"Help!"

Wren wiggled her toes in her skates. Slowly she brought her knees to her chest and wrapped her arms tight.

She didn't dare move anything else.

Wren thought about the shiny, dense ice of the Dartmouth College rink. Sitting next to Charlie on the hard bench of his Zamboni machine. Back then, she'd been so certain that one day she'd stand on a podium. And everyone would be so proud.

But now, stuck on this fragile ice in the dark, Wren thought about something else that happened at the rink that year. Nancy had tried to start a synchronized skating team. She'd gathered her students and shown them a video of a team from Connecticut that did back crossovers with their arms linked and deep lunges in between one another's outstretched arms. Nancy had lined them up by height to try to repeat what the Connecticut girls had done.

And Wren had hated it. She didn't want to count in unison as she did back crossovers or be responsible for steadying someone else's balance in a spiral.

The other girls' hands pressing on her shoulders just slowed her down.

Wren wanted space to build her crossovers. To launch into her jumps. To twist into her layback spins.

Unlike the rest of her life, when Wren was skating, no one could drag her down. There was no Hannah to worry about. To talk about. To plan around. No Nora to offend. No Izzy to scare away.

When Wren was on the ice, she could accomplish amazing things all by herself.

And now look what she'd done.

All by herself.

The shore wasn't far, but she didn't have the courage to move toward it. What if the ice cracked completely and she fell through? Would the cold water instantly stop her heart?

The thought made her chest tight. Her breath short.

Wren could only sit and wait.

And wonder if she was going to die.

Then she heard a rustling through the trees. A familiar voice. "Wren! Wren! Are you there?"

It was Izzy. She was running to the edge of the ice, waving her arms.

Yes, thought Wren. *I'm here*. But when she opened her mouth to speak, the words scratched against her throat and faded to nothing.

"Hold on," said Izzy. "I'm coming to get you."

Izzy tested the ice with her foot. She frowned,

walked a few steps away, and tested another spot.

"I don't know," yelled Izzy. "Maybe I should go get our moms. They're home. I told them I'd be right back."

"No!" It took every bit of strength for Wren to yell the word. Izzy couldn't leave her. *Please don't go.*

"Okay," said Izzy. "Okay, I'll stay. But can you try to come in? Do you think you can do it?"

Izzy crouched at the edge of the ice and stretched her arms toward Wren. She wasn't close to reaching, but she was there. Izzy had found her. Wren had to try.

Wren shifted onto all fours. She pressed her palms flat on the ice, her fingers spread wide, covering the cracks like Band-Aids.

Band-Aids that Wren wasn't sure would stick.

"You can do it," said Izzy. "Go slow."

Go slow. The words echoed in Wren's mind as she began to move.

Right hand, left hand. Right knee, left knee. Wren was careful to keep her toe picks clear of the ice. To slide, not thump.

"You're doing it," said Izzy. "Keep going."

The splintered surface with its cracks and grooves was terrifying. But Izzy kept her going.

"You're almost there," said Izzy. "Come on, Wren. You've got this."

Right hand, left hand. Slide.

Wren was close. But as she shifted forward, the ice underneath her hands gave way.

Frigid water seeped over her knuckles. Her wrists.

Wren gasped.

Her palms hit the hard-packed mud bottom of the pond.

The water was cold and sharp as it rushed up to her elbows. Wren's body clenched tight.

But when she looked up, Izzy was on her hands and knees. Coming to get her.

IZZY'S IMPOSSIBLY
BIG THING

Izzy crawled a few inches before the ice at the edge of the pond cracked. But she knew from Row splashing in during the summer that the water was shallow this close to shore. Izzy braced herself for the cold and stepped in, wading toward Wren. As she approached, Wren reached up and Izzy slid her arms beneath Wren's shoulders. Together they made their way out of the pond and collapsed on the sandy dirt.

Wren's feet splayed open and the wet blades of her skates shone in the moonlight. The wavy glow of white moon on steel was beautiful, except that Izzy was panting too hard to appreciate it. She dropped her chin to her chest, taking comfort in the rise and fall of her body. They were both all right. At least, she hoped so.

"Are you okay?" Izzy asked Wren.

Wren nodded, her lips a deep purple.

Izzy's breath began to slow and she leaned forward to lift the clinging wet denim material from her lower calves. She wiggled her toes inside her soaked boots. When Izzy sat back up, Wren made a noise, as if clearing her throat to speak.

"Thanks for saving my life," whispered Wren.

Izzy didn't know how to answer. *You're welcome? No problem?* Had she really saved Wren's life? It seemed an impossibly big thing to do. But before Izzy had found her, Wren was trapped in the center of the ice. And now here they were. Together and safe.

But before Izzy could answer, voices called from the direction of the path. "Izzy! Wren! Girls!"

"Mom," said Wren in a raspy voice.

"Down here!" yelled Izzy. "We're down here!"

In a flurry of rustling leaves and pounding steps, their moms appeared at the opening to the path and wrapped them both in hugs. Izzy's mom kissed her cheek, her forehead, her cheek again. Then she pulled away, noticing Izzy's wet legs and jacket sleeves. "Did you fall in?"

"Wren's soaked," said Wren's mom. "That water must be freezing. I should take her to a doctor—Izzy, too."

Izzy's mom reached her hand over to Wren's cheek. "You're right. Better to be safe. There's an emergency room in the next town over. Come on."

Izzy stood, her arms wrapped tight around her body, as her mom and Wren's mom helped Wren up. Wren grimaced, releasing a small wheezing sound.

"Your skates," said Izzy. "Do you want to take them off?"

"No," said Wren. "Please . . ."

"It's okay," said Wren's mom. "I've got her." With one smooth motion, she wrapped Wren's arm around her neck and slid her hands underneath Wren's body, lifting Wren as if she weighed nothing at all.

Izzy reached for her mom's hand and followed them up the path. With each step, moisture squished between her toes and under the soles of her feet. Her jeans clung to her legs and the sleeves of her jacket twisted around her arms. Outside, Izzy was shivering with cold. But inside, her mom's fingers squeezing her palm, she was warm. Opposites.

WREN SEES THE LIGHT

A knock on the sticker door.

Wren opened her eyes. The bed was so cozy, so familiar, that for a second she forgot what had happened last night.

But then Wren moved her arm. The bandage where the IV needle had been inserted brushed against the sheets. And it all came rushing back.

The icy cold. The heated blanket. The oxygen monitor tight over her finger.

"Come in," she said.

The sticker door swung open. Izzy flopped down

at the end of the bed. "Were you still sleeping?" she asked.

Wren looked to the window. A bright midday winter sun shone around the curtain edges. "What time is it?"

"Almost noon," said Izzy. "Isn't that great!"

"Great?" Wren's head ached. The doctor had warned her about that. She remembered something about staying hydrated.

"We missed theater camp," continued Izzy. "Even my mom didn't have the energy to get up this morning. I mean, I know you almost died. But at least something good came out of it."

Izzy smiled. But then the corners of her mouth dropped. "Sorry," said Izzy. "I didn't mean . . ."

"Anytime," said Wren. She did a pretend bow, like Otto might, one arm at her waist and the other outstretched as if holding a tray.

Izzy laughed. And so did Wren. The shaking made her head hurt. But it was so worth it.

Except then Wren remembered there was

something else she needed to say and she stopped laughing. She should have said it in the hospital last night. But she and Izzy had been taken to different exam rooms. And when they were released, at almost two in the morning, Izzy fell asleep as soon as they got in the car.

But now, Wren had no excuse. "I'm sorry for what I said about you not having any friends."

Izzy bit her lower lip. She hesitated. "The thing is, it's kind of the truth."

"No," said Wren. "Not anymore."

Izzy shifted on the bed. Crossed her legs underneath her. She spun the hospital ID bracelet, the same kind that Wren had, around her wrist. Then Izzy stood up and reached into the back pocket of her jeans.

"Here," she said. "This is for you. It's from Daphne."

"Daphne?" asked Wren, feeling bumps in the envelope. "Is there poison inside? Because almost dying once is enough for me."

Izzy shook her head. "It's an invitation. Open it."

Wren pulled out a piece of paper the same color as

the envelope. She held the paper so Izzy could see, but Izzy barely glanced at the words before turning away.

It was an invitation to an epic sleepover at Daphne's house. But why would Daphne ever invite her?

Confused, Wren pulled out the other item in the envelope: a red beaded bracelet.

Izzy gasped. She leaned over and touched the bracelet with one finger.

"What's wrong?" asked Wren.

"I think it's a setup," said Izzy. Izzy explained how Phoebe's and Serena's envelopes had bracelets with tie-dye beads. "Daphne probably wants you to come so she can turn you away at the door. She probably didn't think I would see you open the envelope. She really is the queen of mean."

"But there's no way I would ever go to her sleepover," said Wren. "Never ever."

"That's not the way Daphne thinks. She thinks everyone wants to hang out with her, no matter what."

Wren nodded in agreement.

The question was: What to do about it?

IZZY'S IDEA

The next afternoon, Saturday, Izzy went back to hang out with Wren. She sat at her desk, doodling on a piece of paper. Wren was stretched out on Izzy's bed, her bag of clothes packed and waiting by the closet. Wren's mom and dad were at the hospital with Hannah. Wren and her dad were going to drive back to New Hampshire right after dinner. Wren's mom would sleep at the hospital and bring Hannah home in a few days.

"We can't let them get away with this," said Wren. She picked up the techno blue envelope next to her on the bed.

"She's Daphne," said Izzy. "She gets away with everything. It's the way life works."

Wren slid the red beaded bracelet over her hand so that it stacked on top of her hospital ID bracelet. "Do you have any scissors?" she asked. "This hospital bracelet is so annoying. I need to cut it off."

Izzy looked at her own hospital ID bracelet. It was embarrassing, too embarrassing to admit to Wren, but Izzy wished Wren would keep hers on just a little while longer. She liked the way they matched.

Still, Izzy got the scissors from her desk and brought them to Wren on the bed. She was about to hand the scissors to Wren when she froze. Their matching hospital bracelets, the red beaded bracelet, the invitation to the epic sleepover, her butterfly tin of Sharpies on the desk.

They were dots that connected to form a plan.

"Wait a second," said Izzy. "I have an idea."

Two hours later, Nate backed down the driveway with Wren and Izzy in the backseat. "We need some music," said Nate. "Something doomed, because you two are up to no good."

"Just drive, Nate," said Izzy.

She and Wren had thought about walking. But the sun had already set and there was no way their parents were going to let them wander out in the dark anytime soon. So they'd convinced Nate to take them out for pizza before Wren left for New Hampshire with her dad. With just one quick stop first.

"Over there," said Izzy, pointing to Daphne's house. "The house with the lights."

"Be fast," said Nate. "I've got a date."

"A date?" asked Izzy.

"A date with destiny. If my little sister can save someone's life, I can ask a girl out. At least if I make it before closing time." Izzy smiled. She wanted to say something cheesy like "Way to go," or "I know she's going to say yes." But she was too nervous about what she and Wren were about to do. She'd have plenty of time to talk to Nate. Her time with Wren was almost up.

Lights glowed through the windows of Daphne's

house. Izzy couldn't see Daphne, Phoebe, and Serena inside, but she felt a buzz in the air knowing they were there. Nate pulled to the curb and turned off the engine.

"Okay," said Wren. "Let's do this."

Wren got out of the car and walked up the stone path that led to Daphne's front door. Izzy followed, stepping off the path and into the shadows by some bushes. Her body shook with nerves as Wren continued up to the front door and reached for the doorbell.

Ding-dong.

Daphne appeared right away, as if she'd been standing in the front hall waiting for this very moment. "Oh, hey, Wren," she said with a big smile. "Are you here for the sleepover?"

"Awesome," said Phoebe, who appeared next to Wren.

Waiting in the dark, Izzy's legs felt soft, like she might collapse. She was tempted to hobble out, tap Wren on the shoulder, and drag her away before they went any further. But then Wren said the exact line that they'd rehearsed in Izzy's bedroom that afternoon, both of them laughing as they tried different voices, joking that Mr. Blair would finally be proud of them for adding emotion to their words.

"Thanks so much for inviting me to your epic sleepover," said Wren in the happy tone they'd settled on. "I have my bracelet."

"Perfect," said Daphne. "Can I see it? Obviously it's your ticket to come inside."

"Sure," said Wren.

Izzy took a few cautious steps onto the grass. She watched as Wren pushed up the sleeve to her jacket. On Wren's wrist was her hospital ID bracelet with four letters written in crisp black Sharpie: *N I C E.*

Phoebe shook her head. She crossed her arms over her chest. "That's not the right bracelet, Wren. You have to have the right bracelet."

Daphne stepped closer to Wren, ignoring Phoebe and squinting at Wren's wrist. "'Nice'? Like you want to tell me how nice I am? I mean, thanks, Wren. That's super sweet. But that's not the bracelet that came with your envelope. Do you have that bracelet? Maybe then you can come in."

Wren shook her head, pretending to be confused. "Oh, right," she said, slapping her forehead. "Silly me, I do have another bracelet."

That was Izzy's cue. There was no turning back. Izzy stepped out of the darkness and onto the stone path. She moved slowly at first, but as she got closer, Izzy saw the confusion in Phoebe's and Daphne's eyes. She saw Serena standing on the stairs holding a fat black cat with white paws. Izzy stepped next to Wren and pushed up her own jacket sleeve. Written on her hospital ID bracelet in black Sharpie were the letters *T R Y*.

Daphne looked from Wren's bracelet to Izzy's bracelet. "Nice? Try?"

Serena put the cat down and stepped forward. She read both bracelets out loud and laughed.

"What does that even *mean*?" asked Phoebe.

"Come on, Phoebe," said Izzy. "I know you can figure it out."

Phoebe stuck out her lower lip. She looked from the bracelets to Daphne.

Daphne hesitated. She flipped her hair. Then she opened her mouth to speak. "It means that . . ."

But Izzy didn't let Daphne finish. "It means that you can do whatever you want with my drawing. I know who you are and so does everyone else. Come on, Wren. Let's go."

Izzy grabbed Wren's hand and they ran to Nate's waiting car. It was just like the night they chased after Row, how they'd sprinted together through the dark, laughing at nothing except the thrilling combination of excitement and fear and hope.

Maybe Nate had been right when he said that her drawings were missing something.

Maybe what they were missing was not one superhero, but two.

TWO
WEEKS
LATER

WREN'S KEY CHAIN

Wren shook out her legs. She stretched her hands over her head.

There was one skater left. Then it would be her turn to take the ice at sectionals.

Wren glanced up several rows to where Hannah, her dad, and her mom sat in small plastic seats. Hannah waved her stuffed unicorn in the air. She wore a pink fuzzy hat that protected the stitches on her head. She looked just like any other healthy, unicorn-loving four-year-old. Which, thanks to the successful surgery, she was.

Wren's dad mouthed, "You've got this, Bird."

Her mom pulled her arms in tight, reminding Wren about what she'd been practicing that week with her double lutz.

Wren nodded. She wiggled her toes in her new skates. Her old ones, which were perfectly broken in, had been lost somewhere in the hospital. Probably stuffed in a trash can with all kinds of needles and bandages. Wren was bummed that she never got a chance to say good-bye.

It had taken a few days to get used to her new skates. She'd worn them around the house, even eating dinner with them on, and now they felt just right.

"Almost time," said Nancy.

Wren got her water bottle from her skating bag and took a sip. Before Wren left, she and Izzy exchanged hospital bracelets. Wren had attached Izzy's bracelet with the word *TRY* to the handle of her skating bag, like a key chain.

A reminder of a week that she never expected to want to remember.

The skater on the ice finished her program.

Wren's name echoed across the empty stretch of ice.

Nancy lifted Wren's chin. She looked Wren in the eyes. "Go out there and show them what you've got."

Wren skated to center ice and got into her opening position. As she waited for her music to start, Wren glanced at the seats next to her family.

Izzy and her mom were sitting very straight, their arms linked. Izzy smiled and gave Wren a thumbs-up.

Wren would do this next part on her own.

But knowing they were all there watching gave Wren strength.

And when she landed her double lutz, she could hear them cheer.

IZZY MAKES ROOM

Two days after Wren's skating competition, Izzy stood in the front yard of her house. The blue car was still parked in the driveway. "No, Row," said Izzy. "We can't go inside yet."

Her mom was meeting with the potential client who'd cancelled three weeks before, and Izzy was supposed to keep Row out of the house until she left. But then Row noticed a squirrel climbing up the maple tree in the front yard. Row lunged, and his leash slipped out of Izzy's grip.

"Row!" yelled Izzy. She ran to the tree and grabbed

the end of Row's leash. "No, Row. Bad dog."

Izzy led Row, his tail wagging with pride, to the back door. She sat down on the step. The sun was strong and Izzy closed her eyes. Flashes of tangerine orange and bright yellow appeared behind her eyelids. As soon as she got back inside, she'd practice mixing the different yellows of her new oil pastels. She liked how oil pastels blended on paper to create shadows, texture, and depth.

Her life was more complicated now than Sharpie stick figures shouting words trapped inside speech bubbles. It was opposites—good and bad, easy and hard, best friends and sworn enemies—and also everything in between.

"Hey, Izzy," said a voice.

Izzy opened her eyes, surprised to see Serena standing in front of her.

"What are you doing here?"

"My mom's meeting with your mom," said Serena. "Your mom invited me in, but I told her I'd just wait in the car."

"Your mom is Ms. Stallton?" asked Izzy. Serena's last name was Tallis.

"She goes by her maiden name now," said Serena. "My parents are getting divorced and my mom wants a totally clean start. With everything. And just so you know, I wasn't avoiding you. I just didn't feel like coming inside and listening to our moms talk about bathroom tiles and window curtains, like they're going to magically fix everything."

Izzy smiled. "Do not get my mom started on curtains."

Serena laughed and kicked a pebble with her sneaker. "Hey, Izzy?"

"Yeah?"

"I'm sorry. About everything with Daphne. I didn't know about the red bracelet trick until the day of the sleepover when you and Wren didn't show up to theater camp. Daphne spent the entire day worrying that her plan would fall apart. So I thought there was a good chance that Wren wouldn't even come to the sleepover. I probably shouldn't have gone anyways, but my mom was home packing boxes and anything was better than doing that. And also, I just didn't want to be left out."

Izzy nodded. She remembered walking with Phoebe's pink mitten in her hand, ringing the doorbell at Daphne's house, and hoping that Daphne would invite her inside.

"I always knew Daphne was mean," continued Serena. "But I didn't know how much she liked being mean until that night."

"It's her specialty," said Izzy. "She's the queen of mean. That's what Otto says."

"Otto makes me laugh," said Serena.

"Me, too," said Izzy.

"Maybe we could all sit together at lunch or something?"

Izzy smiled. "Yeah."

Serena's mom opened the back door, bags of colorful fabric samples in her hand. Izzy brought Row inside and went up to her room. She pressed her forehead against the window, watching as Serena and her mom backed down the driveway. Her breath did not cloud the glass. There was no condensation heart to slice in half with her finger.

Izzy sat down at her desk and opened the drawer. Her jagged half-heart necklace was shoved in the back, the chain a tangled mess. Over the past two weeks, Izzy had been tempted to throw it out, but she never did. Instead, she put Wren's hospital ID bracelet with the word *NICE* in the necklace's old place.

The bracelet had wrinkled at the edges and curled in on itself. The opposite of the flat, shiny heart.

But Izzy didn't care how the bracelet looked. She knew what the bracelet *meant*. And she also knew there was plenty of empty space beside it for whatever might come next.

ACKNOWLEDGMENTS

Thank you to my editor, Martha Mihalick, for being a true partner in shaping this story. It is a joy and an honor to write with you.

Thank you to my agent, Alex Slater, for believing in me every step of the way. I'm so grateful to be on your team.

Thank you to the incredible people at Greenwillow Books. To Virginia Duncan for the caring and insightful comments, Tim Smith for indulging my debates over comma placement, Sylvie Le Floc'h for the gorgeous pages, and the entire marketing, publicity, and sales teams for working so hard to get this book and so many others into the hands of readers. And to artist Celia Krampien for the beautiful cover and interior art.

There are so many wonderful pediatric doctors and nurses who have brightened my toughest days. For specific medical advice on this book, I was fortunate to rely on Dr. Ann McCarthy and Dr. Vishnu Cuddapah. Any mistakes are mine alone.

Thank you to the librarians who hand my books to readers, the teachers who recommend them to students, the booksellers who present them to customers, and the young readers who write to me. Hearing from you makes me smile for days.

To my brothers, Alex and Ben Ende, all the sibling love in these pages goes out to you.

Endless hugs and kisses to my daughters: Ella, Liv, and Aven. You girls are the heart of everything I write. And to Winnie, the real-life Row who we love so very much.

This book is dedicated to my husband, Jeff. As everything I write should be.

Where do young pop stars, movie stars, princesses, and geniuses go to get away from all the cameras?

To a summer camp exclusively for them!

But what happens when an ordinary girl ends up there for the summer?

Read on for an excerpt from *Camp Famous!*

Can the most ordinary girl in the world fit in at . . .

CAMP
FAMOUS

JENNIFER BLECHER

I started getting ready for Camp Summerah right away. Mom printed the packing list from her email, and I taped it above my desk. I placed neat check marks with my purple fluff pen next to the items as I collected them: bug spray, flashlight, shower caddy, laundry bag.

The Camp Summerah packing list was almost identical to the Camp Longatocket packing list, which was a good sign. I still didn't know very much about Camp Summerah. Ms. McIntyre clearly didn't like talking about camp at school. But when no one else was nearby, she would answer some of my questions about the activities they offered, the number of girls in a cabin, the food. And whenever I thanked her for getting me a spot, she would hug me and promise that it was going be "a life-changing summer."

I was so ready for my life to change.

I stacked my piles of shirts, shorts, underwear, socks, and other clothes in the corner of my room. If I wore something to school, I removed it from the pile and then added it right back after it was washed. The neat stacks were the last thing I saw at night and the first thing I saw in the morning. They made camp feel closer. Something physical to remind me that my dream was actually coming true.

Finally, after weeks of waiting, it was time to lift my piles from the floor and place them in a large navy duffel bag. I put my notebook in my backpack next to some paperback books for the plane ride. At the last minute, I decided to bring my pig eraser, Wilbur, as well.

Wilbur reminded me of Quinn, but also of Marin. I didn't want the Quinn part of my life to come with me to camp, but I liked bringing the Marin part.

Marin was a friend magnet. When she'd opened her palm that morning at school, she wasn't just giving me a pig eraser in a pile of other animal erasers; she was giving me a sympathy hug.

Maybe I could do the same for someone at camp?

My hand shook as I dropped Wilbur into the front pocket of my backpack and zipped it closed. I wanted only to be excited, but there was so much to worry about. What if giving someone a used pig eraser was weird?

It probably was, right? Like, super weird.

I was about to take Wilbur out of my backpack and place him back on my desk when Dad appeared at my door. "Our ride is coming in ten minutes. You ready?"

I nodded. "Ready."

Dad and I each took a handle of the duffel bag and carried it down the stairs. Dad groaned as he hoisted the bag next to the large suitcases already waiting on the front steps for the ride to the airport.

Mom and Dad were going on a bird-watching trip in the desert for one of Dad's magazine assignments. While I had been stacking T-shirts and shorts in my bedroom, they had been laying out camping equipment, binoculars, and matching khaki vests with loaded pockets on the dining room table.

Mom never went on assignment with Dad. But since I was going to be away at sleepover camp, she'd asked for time off from work. She'd been collecting hardback novels from the library for weeks.

My parent's flight to the desert left a few hours after my flight to Camp Summerah, so we all went to the airport together. As we drove away from our house, Mom reached over and squeezed my hand. I squeezed back once before pulling my hand away and sliding it under my thighs.

I wanted to skip this whole part. Saying good-bye to my parents. The airplane ride to a small airport in Vermont, where a counselor would be waiting for me with a "Camp Summerah" sign that said my name.

I just wanted to be at camp already.

I looked out the car window as Mom and Dad repeated all the things that I already knew. They would be out of cell phone range, so I should call Grandma in case of emergency. They would be thinking of me the entire time and knew I was going to have an amazing experience. They trusted me to make the right decisions and always be kind.

By the time we arrived at the airport, even the driver seemed sick of hearing it.

"Well," said Dad as we unloaded our bags. "This is quite the hullaballoo."

That was Dad-talk for busy and hectic. Which it was. Photographers were standing in a tight pack outside the sliding glass doors, pointing their long-lensed cameras toward the check-in area.

"What's going on?" I asked

Mom ignored me, but a photographer answered my question. "Camp Famous," he said. "The kids should be arriving any minute."

"What's Camp Famous?"

The photographer lowered his camera and shook his head, as if it was the dumbest question he'd ever heard. "Where the most famous kids in the world go to sleepover camp. The place is in nowheresville and strictly off-limits. No helicopter flyovers, no speedboat drive-bys, no drones. This is the last glimpse we're gonna get of the famous kids for three weeks. That means both me and my bank account need this shot. So move along."

I was confused, and also kind of offended, when suddenly the cameras started click, click, clicking. The noise reminded me of that unfortunate time in kindergarten when my parents forced me to take tap dance lessons. It was fast and furious, echoing off the hard surfaces of the airport.

"Come on, Abby," said Mom, grabbing me by the elbow. "Let's check our bags and get to the gate."

I followed my parents to the airline counter, rising onto my tiptoes to try and get a look at the famous kids. Would they look as nervous about going to Camp Famous as I felt about going to Camp Summerah? But the photographers were a human wall of backs and hunched shoulders. I couldn't see anything other than the occasional flash of light.

"Hullabaloo," said Dad, pulling me toward the security line. "Quite the hullabaloo."

Mom shot him a look. "Exactly."

We passed through security and found an empty corner near my gate. Mom sat down next to me and placed her hand on my arm. She was about to speak when the sound of the famous kids walking down the airport corridor stopped her. They were a slow, steady, graceful thump of cool.

From behind the security check-in at the end of the terminal, photographers called out their names with the desperation of people facing imminent death.

"Isabella!"

"Over here!"

"Cameron!"

"Turn around! One last wave for your fans!"

As the famous kids got closer, Mom's grip on my arm got tighter. She rose from her seat and kneeled on the ground in front of me. "Abby," she said. "I need you to listen to me."

Did she not hear the shouts? Did she not see how close the famous kids were?

I'd been listening to Mom for the entire ride to the airport. For my entire life! I knew everything she had to say. Then Dad kneeled down beside her. He placed one hand on my knee and the other on Mom's shoulder.

What was happening?

"I'm just going to spit it out," said Mom. "Abby, you're not going to Camp Summerah. You're going to Camp Famous."

If Mom had actually spit, if a spray of saliva had landed smack in the center of my eyeballs, I could not have been more surprised.

"What?"

"It's true," said Dad. "You're going to Camp Famous."

I was all for repetition. I'd been playing the same Kai Carter songs for weeks. But in this case, saying the words a second time did not help. Clearly my parents were losing it.

"But we already checked my bag," I said slowly.

"Right. To Camp Famous," said Dad.

"What happened to Camp Summerah?"

Had they gotten a text message or email on the way to the airport? Had Camp Summerah burned down?

"It never existed," said Dad. "I made it up. Clever, right? Like, ah, I love summer. But in reverse. Get it?"

I looked from Dad to Mom. Dad babbled when he was nervous. Mom was the opposite. Nerves focused her. That's why she was so good at arguing cases in court.

Except that Mom seemed similarly rattled, her eyes moving rapidly across my face. "We weren't entirely honest with you, Abby," she said. "But for a good reason. If we'd told you that you were going to Camp Famous, you would have started searching online and read all the tabloid articles about the place. We didn't want to you to get all nervous about going. That's why we're surprising you." Mom hesitated. She did jazz hands. "Surprise!"

Of course I would have gotten all nervous about it! Had they heard what that photographer said? Camp Famous was where the most famous kids in the world went to sleepover camp!

I was the least famous kid in the world. I didn't have a single sports trophy on my bookshelf. Not one shiny ribbon hanging from my door handle. I'd never even had a best friend.

"But what about Ms. McIntyre's brother?" I said. "That's how I got a spot."

"Ms. McInytre's brother runs Camp Famous," said Mom.

Mom's confession was a lollipop after a flu shot. For a second it made me feel better. But then

I realized what it meant: Ms. McIntyre had been lying to me as well. All those times at recess when I'd whispered questions about sleepover camp, she'd answered as if I was going to a normal camp, not a camp for celebrities!

"But I'm not famous. . . . " I trailed off as I caught sight of two famous kids.

The first was Princess Isabella Victoria Montgomery. She had the exact same look of amused boredom as she did on the cover of People magazine, where she'd posed on the front steps of a huge castle wearing a white ball gown and hot pink Converse sneakers. The caption underneath said: "No Glass Slippers for This Modern Princess." A vibe of I-dare-you-to-mess-with-me wafted off the magazine cover.

The second kid I recognized was Kai Carter. Kai Carter! K.C.! He was wearing his signature red sweatshirt and chewing on the drawstrings. His hair swooped across his forehead in one smooth wave. I looked over my shoulder for Marin and

Quinn. Surely they would come racing around the corner, their arms waving, their screams piercing.

Before I could see any other famous kids clearly enough to recognize them, Mom put her hands against my cheeks. She brought her face close to mine. "Abigail, listen to me. This is what you wanted. Sleepover camp. You can do this. Dad and I will be waiting right here when you get back."

Dad kissed the top of my head. "Listen to your mother, Abby. She is very wise."

It was as if I'd been sucked into a tornado. Everything that used to be on solid ground was suddenly swirling. I wrapped my arms around my parents in a combination of excitement and fear. With my arms still locked around their backs, Mom and Dad shuffled me out of our corner spot.

Then I felt Dad lift his arm from my back as if he was waving to someone.

The very last someone I ever expected to see standing among the most famous kids in the world.

☆☆☆